THE Sisters 8

BOOK 4

JACKIE'S JOKES

By Lauren Baratz-Logsted
With Greg Logsted & Jackie Logsted

Illustrated by Lisa K. Weber

sandpiper

HOUGHTON MIFFLIN HARCOURT
BOSTON • NEW YORK • 2009

www.sandpiperbooks.com

SANDPIPER and the SANDPIPER logo are trademarks
of Houghton Mifflin Harcourt Publishing Company.

The text of this book is set in Youbee.
Book design by Carol Chu.

Library of Congress Cataloging-in-Publication Data
Baratz-Logsted, Lauren.
Jackie's jokes / by Lauren Baratz-Logsted
with Greg Logsted and Jackie Logsted
p. cm. — (The sisters eight ; bk. 4)
Summary: April Fools' Day is long and hard
for the third-grade Huit octuplets, but it
is nothing compared to the challenges
of Tax Day, through which Jackie
discovers her special power and gift
and learns more about their parents'
mysterious disappearance. ISBN
978-0-547-22668-2 (hardcover)
ISBN 978-0-547-05328-8 (pbk.)
[1.   Sisters—Fiction.   2.
April Fools' Day—Fiction.
3.   Practical   jokes—
Fiction. 4. Abandoned
children—Fiction.   5.
Schools—Fiction.]   I.
Logsted,   Greg.   II.
Logsted, Jackie. III.
Title.
PZ7.B22966Jac
2009
[Fic]—dc22

2008036763

Printed in the United
States of America
MP 10 9 8 7 6
5 4 3 2 1

For the Douglas gals:
Kaethe, Veronica, and Natasha

Thank you for being the best invisible
pals a trio of authors could have.
Our work is better because of you.
Long live pink frosting!

Annie   Durinda   Georgia   Jackie

Marcia   Petal   Rebecca   Zinnia

PROLOGUE

Let's recap.

Hmm . . . what's that? You say you don't know what *recap* means?

Oh, dear. First the book is talking to you, and now you're talking to the book. My, but I think you *are* in trouble. Is there perhaps a doctor you should be seeing about that? You know, there are special doctors who can help with all sorts of things.

While you're thinking that over, let me explain that *recap,* which is what I'm about to do, is when a person repeats the main points of something, turning a complicated something into a much clearer something. There are many reasons you might want to do a recap: (1) you might worry your listeners have fallen asleep at some point; (2) you might worry no one was ever really paying attention in the first place; or (3) you might need to remind yourself of all the important points because the story's gotten so confusing, you don't remember where you are anymore, plus you have a feeling something even more important is going to happen soon and you need to know where you've been in order to know where you're going.

I'd ask which reason you think applies here, but you're off seeing that doctor about your little problem, aren't you? So I'll just do my recap now, even if I'm the only one listening. Deep breath. Here goes:

- Eight sisters, octuplets, almost eight, will be eight on August 8, 2008. Named, from oldest to youngest: Annie, Durinda, Georgia, Jackie, Marcia, Petal, Rebecca, Zinnia. Last name: Huit. All with brown hair, brown eyes. Each is one minute older than the next. Each is one inch taller than the next.
- Eight cats, all gray and white puffballs: Anthrax, Dandruff, Greatorex, Jaguar, Minx, Precious, Rambunctious, Zither.
- Magnificent stone home that looks like a castle, crazy rooms, inventions—too bad they don't all work as they ought to.
- New Year's Eve in 2007: Mom (Lucy) goes to kitchen for eggnog, Dad (Robert) goes out for more firewood, neither one comes back. Oh no. This can't be good.
- Note found behind loose stone in drawing room says each sister must find her power

and gift in order to find out what happened to Mommy and Daddy. By the way, Mommy is a scientist and Daddy is a model, so you'd think they'd be able to get out of any jam, but who knows this time.

• Eight little girls, home all alone—that can't be good either.

• Annie's power: can be smart as an adult; Annie's gift: purple ring.

• Durinda's power: can freeze anyone, except Zinnia, by tapping her leg three times rapidly and then pointing sharply at a person; Durinda's gift: green earrings.

• Georgia's power: can make herself invisible by twitching her nose twice; Georgia's gift: a golden compact, which she sent back the first time the carrier pigeon tried to bring it. (Note: Carrier pigeons visit the Eights often. This could be important at some point.)

• Each cat has the same power as the Eight that it belongs to.

• Zinnia thinks that the animals understand her and that she understands them. Everyone else has doubts about this.

• Pete the mechanic, good; Mrs. Pete, good; the Wicket, evil; Crazy Serena, crazy; the McG, better than she was.

• The Eights still love Will Simms, and they like Mandy Stenko better than before.

• Carl the talking refrigerator in love with robot Betty. Well, who wouldn't be?

• Location: Could be the States, could be England, could be somewhere no one has ever heard of. All we do know is that the address is 888 Middle Way.

• The Eights find their powers and gifts at a rate of one sister per month, so Annie found hers in January, Durinda found hers in February, Georgia found hers in March, Jackie—

Oh, look. Fancy that: the calendar page is about to turn, and when it does . . .

Look out, everyone! There's a story coming your way!

Jackie, look out! Your month is about to—

CHAPTER ONE

—Start.

Tuesday, April 1, 2008, approximately five thirty in the morning.

"Annie, Durinda, Georgia, Jackie, Petal, Rebecca, Zinnia—come quick!" Marcia shouted.

Six of us rubbed sleep from our eyes before obeying Marcia's insanely early summons. We weren't supposed to get up for school for another forty minutes. One of the Eights, Jackie, was nowhere to be seen.

We followed Marcia's shouting voice down to the kitchen.

"Look!" she cried, pointing at the window.

"What?" Annie asked. "Is there another pigeon out there with a note?"

"No!" Marcia said excitedly. "Can't you see it? There's a horse's behind right outside the window."

"*What?*" six Eights cried, hurrying to look out the window.

Huh. There was nothing there.

"Happy April Fools' Day!" Marcia gloated with glee.

"Fine. You got us," Rebecca said sourly. "But don't think you can get us again."

"As long as we're all up early," Durinda said, "I may as well start breakfast. Jackie, could you please get me the—Oh dear. Where is Jackie?"

"I can help you with breakfast this morning," Zinnia offered.

"That's great," Durinda said, looking meaningfully at Georgia and Rebecca. "It's always nice when *someone* around here helps out."

"Hey!" Georgia said. "Don't look at me! *I* haven't said anything awful."

"Yet," Annie provided.

"Yet," Georgia admitted with a blush.

"Okay, Zinnia," Durinda directed, "you get the milk out of the fridge—I think we'll make pancakes this morning—while everyone else gets dressed."

Zinnia opened the refrigerator door. The rest of us weren't even out of the room when we heard Carl the talking refrigerator announce: "All out of tasty worms. Must buy more."

"Did Carl just say we needed more tasty worms?" Durinda asked.

Before anyone could answer her, Carl spoke again. "And slugs," he said. "Must buy more juicy slugs."

"Juicy sl—? But we don't eat—"

"And slimy caterpillars," Carl said, cutting Durinda off, "and crunchy dead leaves and hairy spiders and—"

"Oh no!" Petal shrieked. "Carl the talking refrigerator has gone mad! If we follow his shopping instructions and then eat all those awful things, we will all be dead by nightfall! We will—"

"Ha-ha," Carl laughed dryly. "April Fools' on you."

"This is insane." Rebecca was disgusted. "We're even being mocked by our own refrigerator today."

* * * * * * * *

"That's odd," Marcia said as five of us headed back downstairs after we'd gotten dressed. There was still no sign of Jackie. "Durinda and Zinnia said they'd cook breakfast, but I don't smell anything."

We took our places at the table and looked down at our plates. The pancakes didn't look quite right. Annie was the first to try to cut hers, but the fork wouldn't even make a dent. None of us could make a dent.

"I'm starving," Rebecca said, giving up on the fork and resorting to her fingers. But when she went to take a bite—

"Ugh!" she cried. "This pancake isn't made out of pancake! It's made out of rubber!"

"April Fools'!" Durinda and Zinnia shouted, high-fiving each other.

"I don't think it's very funny," Rebecca said. "Some of us are starving here, you know."

"Oh, where's your sense of humor?" Durinda said. Then, when it was clear Rebecca hadn't any, at least not where rubber food was concerned, Durinda added, "Why don't you have some pink frosting?"

"And why don't the rest of us adjourn to the front room while Durinda makes us all some Pop-Tarts?" Annie suggested. "It's about all we have time for now."

"Oh no!" Petal cried as we entered the front room. Then she fainted.

We all looked around to see what had bothered her so, and there it was: Daddy Sparky, the suit of armor we usually dressed up in Daddy's quilted smoking jacket and fedora hat to make nosy parkers believe there was a real man in the house, was wearing Mommy Sally's sleeveless purple dress and pearls, while Mommy Sally, the dressmaker's dummy we dressed up so people would believe there was still a proper lady of the house, was wearing Daddy Sparky's smoking jacket and hat. We must admit, the corncob pipe in her hand looked very elegant there.

"April Fools'?" Annie winced out the words as we

tried to bring Petal around by whispering her name and patting her cheeks softly. Okay, so maybe Rebecca did shout her name . . . and then slap her.

"Wh-wh-wh-what happened?" Petal stammered, coming back to life.

"This is *your* doing?" Rebecca rounded on Annie.

Annie nodded, meekly for once.

"I'm shocked, I tell you," Rebecca said, "simply shocked. I'd expect such behavior from Georgia and, well, from me, of course, but *you?* You're supposed to be the eldest, you're supposed to be in charge, you must have known such a trick would be too much for Petal, who is always so—"

"All *right,*" Annie said through gritted teeth. She'd felt guilty for a moment, but she certainly wasn't going to go on feeling that way forever. "Zinnia," Annie instructed, "why don't you take Petal to the bathroom and, oh, I don't know, put a cold washcloth on her face?"

So that's what Zinnia and Petal did.

There was still no sign of Jackie.

* * * * * * * *

Rebecca's mood was not improved when Georgia put on a monster mask and then leaped out from around a corner and shouted, "Boo!" right in Rebecca's face.

Rebecca nearly went through the roof, in more ways than one.

"April Fools'!" Georgia laughed, removing the mask.

"This whole house has gone insane," Rebecca muttered. "Am I the only one left here who has any sense?"

And Rebecca's mood really didn't improve any when Petal and Zinnia returned, all excited.

"What's wrong?" Annie asked immediately, for Petal and Zinnia were so excited, they couldn't even speak. Well, at least Petal wasn't fainting anymore.

"Come quick!" Zinnia at last gasped out the words.

"Yes!" Petal blurted. "Come quick! The cats are going crazy!"

Not that this was anything new. It seemed as though our cats were always going crazy. Someone breaks into the house while we're out at a party? Cats go crazy. Someone steals Mommy's Top Secret folder from her private study? Cats go crazy. Too much fruitcake smell in the air? Cats go really crazy. Honestly, those cats were hysterical so often, they might as well have been Petal.

As it turned out, when seven of us entered the cat room (which is like our drawing room, only for cats), the cats weren't going crazy at all. In fact, they looked downright peaceful.

"Are you sure they're going crazy?" Marcia asked, one

eyebrow raised. "It looks to me like they're practically sleeping."

It was true. Anthrax, Dandruff, Greatorex, Minx, Precious, Rambunctious, and Zither—they were all curled up together like one giant ball of gray and white yarn.

"Well, yes," Petal said hurriedly, "they do look peaceful *now*—"

"Actually," Zinnia said, cutting her off, "they never looked *not* peaceful, but—"

"But Zinnia heard them all talking," Petal said, "and they were saying they heard that the Wicket returned last night."

The Wicket was our evil neighbor, stealer of Top Secret folders everywhere, who back in February we'd tricked into going to Beijing by making her think that Mommy had taken her secret to eternal life and fled there. We'd long been worrying about her return; the Wicket's, that is.

"Is this true?" Annie demanded of Zinnia.

"Of course it's not true," Georgia said.

"Exactly," Rebecca agreed. "Everyone except Zinnia knows that the cats don't really talk to Zinnia, nor do the cats understand her."

"Oh, but that's exactly what the cats said," Petal said. "You see, this time, I heard them too."

"You did?"

All eyes were on Petal.

"Oh yes," Petal said, practically hopping from foot to foot. It was hard to tell if she was excited, nervous, or had simply failed to use the bathroom when she'd gone in there with Zinnia. "And what's more, Zinnia and I also heard the cats talking amongst themselves, and they're plotting to . . . they're plotting to . . . they're plotting to . . ."

"Plotting to *what?*" Rebecca snapped.

"They're plotting to take over the house!" Petal burst out at last.

"*What?*" Annie said. "This is serious."

"But they are only cats," Marcia observed.

"There's no such thing as 'only cats,'" said Durinda, who took her Dandruff very seriously. "That's like saying we're 'only eight little girls home all alone.' As if we have no power. As if we don't count. As if—"

"Cut the drama," Rebecca said to Durinda. Then she glared at Petal and Zinnia. "You two, tell us all about the kitty coup."

But Petal and Zinnia couldn't tell us that or anything else. They were too busy laughing so hard, they were nearly crying.

"Kitty coup," Petal finally gasped. "April Fools'!"

Petal, who'd never played a practical joke on anybody in her life, looked particularly pleased with herself.

There was still no sign of Jackie.

Come to think of it, there was no sign of her cat, Jaguar, either.

* * * * * * * *

"Ta-da!"

At last, Jackie was back among us. The only problem was . . .

"Your hair!" Rebecca shrieked.

"Happy April Fools' Day!" Jackie trumpeted.

"But cutting your hair is no practical joke," Rebecca said. "It's certainly not a temporary one. So let me point out, once more"—and here she started to shriek again, biting off each word—"You! Cut! Off! Your! Hair!"

"Not all of it," Jackie said, bobbing the tips of her new short hair.

In fact, her new haircut was a bob—short, straight, parted in the middle—which was very different from her usual look: long hair. It did take getting used to.

"Don't you like it?" Jackie asked, but she didn't look worried about our opinion. We could tell she was pleased with what she'd done.

"I . . . *think* I do," Petal said, walking in a wide circle around Jackie. "But however did you manage it?"

"Simple." Jackie shrugged. "I went to the haircutting room."

"The haircutting room?" Petal reeled back in horror. In truth, we all reeled back in horror, all except Annie. Annie was the only one brave enough to go by herself into the haircutting room, where scissors flew around your head like crazy and you never knew if you might lose an ear. The rest of us hadn't gone in there since Mommy had disappeared. Or died.

"You went in there all by yourself?" Petal gulped. It was obvious Petal couldn't think of a scarier thing in the world for a person to do. At least not right that minute. But give our Petal five more minutes, and she'd think of something new to be scared to death over.

"Of course I didn't go alone," Jackie said, "not entirely." Then Jackie placed her thumb and forefinger in the corners of her mouth and let out a loud whistle.

Jaguar came running and threw her little gray and white body straight into Jackie's open arms.

Turned out, Jaguar had had a haircut too.

"Your cat is practically bald," Rebecca said.

"No, she's not." Jackie finally looked offended, and she hugged Jaguar a little closer, stroking her furry chin. "She just has less hair now than all of your cats. So she'll stand out more. It will be very nice for her."

"And now you'll stand out more too," Rebecca said, not looking at all pleased. "Just like your cat, now you have shorter hair than the rest of us."

"Not true," Marcia pointed out. Sometimes, it was as though she had rulers where the rest of us had eyes. "Annie's is still shorter, by a smidge."

"Plus," Georgia added, "Jackie's looks more . . . oh, I don't know . . . *French*."

"It is elegant," Zinnia said.

"Yes, it is," Petal agreed. "I can see that now that I have survived my initial horror."

"Well, *I* don't think it's elegant," Rebecca said.

"Why don't you tell us how you really feel, Rebecca?" Annie said with a heavy sigh. "We've already missed the bus, and we'll have to call Pete for a ride to school because I certainly can't let people see me pull up there in the purple Hummer."

"I think it *stinks!*" Rebecca said.

"May I ask why?" Jackie asked, peacefully enough.

"Because you're not supposed to change anything about yourself," Rebecca at last admitted. "None of us are."

Then Jackie did something that surprised us all: she laughed.

"What are you talking about, you silly girl?" Jackie asked Rebecca. "Not ever change? But I'm not Peter Pan! None of us are! Of course we can change. Even you can change something about yourself if you want to . . . and not just your hair either."

But Rebecca was in no mood for change, hers or anyone else's, as she made clear with a huffy "Well, while Annie calls Pete to come get us, *I'm* going to the drawing room to get my backpack—you know, the one with the *same* pattern I get *every* year."

And then she was gone. Of course, we did have Jackie back, so we figured we were ahead, or at least even.

* * * * * * * *

"Everyone, come quick!" we heard Rebecca's voice shout from the drawing room a moment later.

We had heard a lot of people calling us to come quick that morning, and nothing had turned out to be worth rushing for, but we went quickly now anyway. A person could never tell when speed might actually be required.

In the drawing room we found Rebecca pointing at a stone in the wall. Whoever was leaving us notes always left them behind this stone, and it was now loose; a telltale sign that a note was there.

"Pull it out!" Rebecca urged Jackie. "I'll bet anything that it's your gift arriving early—just like what happened with Georgia!"

"Ooh, your gift!" Zinnia said. "I'll bet it will be something grand!" She sighed heavily. "I wish it were mine."

A gift? Who could resist such a thing? Not even Jackie. Okay, maybe Georgia could, at least initially, but Georgia was always different. Come to that, we all were.

Jackie went to the loose stone, pulled it all the way out, and . . .

Rebecca's cat, Rambunctious, leaped out, practically knocking her over. When cats are put in small places, they are always eager to get out. We must say, though, this time, it wasn't nearly as funny as it had been when we'd put a cat in the mailbox and surprised the mailperson.

"You are evil," Jackie said to Rebecca.

"I do try," Rebecca said with a grin and then turned serious. "And I never intend to change."

CHAPTER TWO

We loved Pete's flatbed pickup truck. Twice he'd saved us with it, and once he'd used it to drive us to dinner at his and Mrs. Pete's home. His truck was a place of great safety for us, and we were looking forward to being driven to school in style that day. No yellow school bus for us!

But when he honked his horn, the horn sounded funny. Well, we told ourselves as we trooped out to the driveway, people can feel fluey, why can't truck horns? So we were still excited when we got outside and found—

"A white stretch limousine?" Rebecca didn't look happy at the prospect, although we must admit, Pete looked spiffy in the chauffeur's cap he wore with his navy blue T-shirt.

"Don't you like it?" Pete asked.

"Oh, it looks perfectly lovely, Mr. Pete," Petal said hurriedly. We suspected she worried that if we criticized the vehicle, Pete would get offended and leave, and then we'd have to walk to school.

"Sure, limos are lovely," Rebecca said, "but we don't like change. Besides which, we're not rock stars."

"Oh, but you should be," Pete said. "At any rate, I'm afraid the flatbed truck isn't running properly, so I had no other choice today."

See? When we heard that horn, we *knew* there was a sick vehicle somewhere.

"Oh, that is very sad, Mr. Pete," Zinnia said.

"I know I hate it when I'm not running properly," Jackie said.

"Do you think the flatbed will *die?*" Rebecca asked. "Death—now that's something that's going around a lot these days."

Pete took off his chauffeur's cap and threw it to the ground. He looked disgusted, and although we'd seen that expression directed at us from other adults—the McG, Principal Freud, the Wicket, Crazy Serena—Pete had never looked at us like that. He was like our parents in that way.

"Did one of us say something wrong?" Annie asked.

"Rebecca often does," Durinda said.

"It's just that I always assumed that if anyone could take a joke," Pete said, "it'd be you lot."

"A joke?" Marcia wondered, looking around her as though she expected to find a joke hiding near the house, perhaps beneath some of the early flowers that were starting to bud. "Where's the joke?"

"It was the idea that there might be something wrong with the flatbed truck," Pete said. "I'm Pete!" he added, as if we didn't know. "I own Pete's Repairs and Auto Wrecking! Of course there's nothing wrong with *my own vehicle!* If there were and I couldn't fix it, what kind of mechanic would I be? Personally, I thought it was probably the greatest April Fools' joke ever."

We immediately saw the error of our ways.

"We are sorry, Mr. Pete," Annie said.

"We should have gotten the joke right away," Durinda said.

"Of course we know you're an ace mechanic," Georgia said.

"Really," Jackie said, "we talk about your mechanical skills all the time."

"I guess we just never pegged you as the practical-joke sort," Marcia said.

"But now that you've explained it to us," Petal said, "we think it's a most excellent joke, even better than pretending that a bunch of cats are about to stage a hostile takeover!" Then she added a nervous "hee-hee."

"We hate practical jokes," Rebecca said.

"Not all of us," Zinnia said. Then she picked up Pete's

cap from the ground, brushed it off for him, and, when he bent down slightly, placed it on his head. "That cap really does look spiffy on you."

"Thanks, Eights," Pete said, and we could tell he appreciated how bad we felt about hurting his feelings, which we would never want to do and not merely because he was the only adult we felt we could wholly trust. "But criminy," he added, "the missus never gets my jokes either."

* * * * * * * *

By the time we got to the Whistle Stop, Pete was in a better mood and so were we. Although we did love the flatbed truck better, we could see where the limo had its advantages: when Pete pulled up in front of the school, he opened the sunroof and let us, one by one, stick our heads out the top and wave to the other students as though we really were rock stars.

"Need me to pick you up after school?" Pete offered.

"Oh no, thank you, Mr. Pete," Petal said, still breathless from her turn through the open sunroof. "I don't think my heart could stand the excitement twice in one day."

"As you wish," Pete said. "So, you know, study hard, Eights. Make something of yourselves."

Good old Pete.

"Oh," he added as we hopped out, "and try not to get yourselves into too much trouble today."

"How do you mean?" Jackie asked.

"Oh, you know," he said, "with it being April Fools' Day and all. Too many jokes can get a person in a peck of trouble." He keyed the ignition. "Oh, and, Jackie?"

"Yes, Mr. Pete?"

"Nice hair."

* * * * * * *

In our classroom, Will Simms and Mandy Stenko looked awfully excited, which was odd, since they were rarely excited about the same things.

Mandy had red hair, which she loved, while Will had white-blond hair, which *we* loved.

"Mrs. McGillicuddy says we're to have recess all day!" Mandy said.

"Oh yes," Will said. "She says we've been so good lately, we deserve an entire day of play." Will looked at us closely before adding, "Nice hair, Jackie."

We looked at the McG. There she was, as always, in all her tall thinness, blond hair, and long nose holding up her glasses.

"Is it true?" Jackie asked for all of us.

"Yes," the McG said simply.

"Really?" Jackie pressed.

"Of course not," the McG said. "Do you think I've taken leave of my senses?" She threw back her head, and laughed the loudest laugh we'd ever heard come out of her, and then she and Will and Mandy all shouted at us, "April Fools'!"

We were beginning to think Rebecca was right: this really was getting to be too much.

* * * * * * * *

The morning slipped away as mornings have a tendency to do when you are busy learning about continental drift, and before we knew it, it was time for recess.

"I've got a splendid idea," Jackie said, after she'd called us all into a huddle on the playground. She included Will in the huddle as well. As for Mandy, she was off talking to the McG, no doubt laughing at the joke they'd pulled on us that morning.

Jackie whispered her idea.

"That really is splendid," Will said. "But are you sure you want to include me? After all, I helped play that joke on you this morning."

"Yeah," Annie said, "but you're you."

"And Mandy and the McG are Mandy and the McG," Georgia added.

"So as you can see," Marcia said, "it's hardly the same thing."

"Jokes are always fine," Rebecca said darkly, "until someone gets hurt."

We ignored her.

"Mandy!" Jackie called sweetly across the playground. "Oh, Mandy!"

Mandy's ears perked up, almost like a puppy's does, and she trotted over.

"Yes?" she asked.

"We all thought we'd play soccer today for recess," Jackie told her. "You know: *Will's favorite game?*"

Mandy looked briefly puzzled, and we can't say that we blamed her. We'd told her many times that Will loved soccer and just as many times that he hated it, so she probably no longer knew what the truth was. (Hint: he hated it.)

"Oh, right," she said, her expression brightening after a moment's reflection. "Well, I'll just go get the ball for us then."

For the next half-hour we played soccer as though we'd been born in Brazil.

Well, at least Jackie did.

She bounced the ball off her head several times, kicked it with authority; she even seemed faster than we remembered her being. We began to wonder: could

her new short hair have something to do with her new speed? We swear, it was like she was everywhere at once—offense, defense, goalie—everywhere we looked, there was Jackie.

"That was great," Jackie said after the end-of-recess bell rang. She didn't even look winded.

"Yes, it was," Mandy said, bending down and placing her palms on her knees because she *was* winded. "It was so nice to play Will's favorite game."

"Too bad, then," Jackie said, "that it isn't Will's favorite game."

Then eight voices plus Will's shouted, "April Fools'!"

Which was, of course, when Mandy Stenko burst into tears.

* * * * * * *

We studied Principal Freud's head. Principal Freud was so bald, we wondered if other kids had called him Egghead when he was younger. Then we felt bad for being mean, not least because being mean was what had landed us in this mess in the first place.

Twelve of us were crammed into Principal Freud's tiny office: we Eights, the McG, Will, Principal Freud, and Mandy, who was still sobbing, although she was sobbing more quietly now. We couldn't see her face because she had it covered with her hands.

"Fancy seeing you all in here," Principal Freud said, only he wasn't looking at the other three when he said this; he was looking at us.

We decided to look at our shoes. They were pretty, for school shoes.

"It seems to me," Principal Freud said, "you're in here a lot now. Why, it's practically become a habit with you."

What was he talking about? We'd only been sent to his office once so far in 2008, and that was back in February, when we'd gotten in trouble for making the McG feel loveless on Valentine's Day. Our record had been clean for a whole month and a half now. Honestly, we'd have expected the statute of limitations to run out on all our other crimes.

"A very bad habit," Principal Freud added darkly.

We looked up out of the corners of our eyes just long enough to see Principal Freud turn his attention to Will. And in that moment, we couldn't even begin to say why, it occurred to us that Principal Freud was not what he'd always appeared to be.

"Will," Principal Freud said to our favorite boy in the world, "while it was wrong of you to participate in these . . . *shenanigans,* I am quite certain you had no part in dreaming them up. You were merely following the poor lead of others."

We stole a glimpse at Will: he didn't look happy. And somehow we knew it had nothing to do with his being labeled a follower, which no one ever really likes, and everything to do with his not wanting to see us hang alone.

"But—" Will started to say. Principal Freud silenced him with a raised palm.

"As for you eight," Principal Freud announced to us, rising from his chair to do so, "you are expelled."

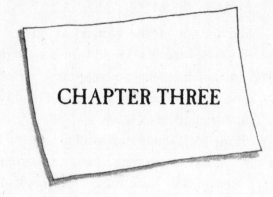

CHAPTER THREE

And then three of the four other people in the room laughed. The McG, Mandy, Principal Freud—they all laughed.

"What's so funny?" Will demanded, outraged. "The Whistle Stop will never be half the place it is now, not even one-*eighth* of the place, without the—"

"Oh, if only you could see your faces!" Principal Freud said between gulping laughs.

"We only pretended to be angry!" the McG said, her laughs somehow fogging up her glasses.

"Of course I knew all along that Will hates soccer!" Mandy said. "Or at least, most of the time I remember that. You all do make it very confusing."

"Does this mean we're not expelled?" Jackie asked.

"Of course not!" Principal Freud said. "Why, if I expelled someone every time they pulled a little harmless prank, there'd be no one left here but me and Mrs. McGillicuddy!"

"Then this was all just . . . ?" Jackie started to say, leaving the end blank for someone else to fill it.

"Yes!" Principal Freud shouted. "April Fools'!"

We were liking him less and less by the minute.

"Oh, and one more thing," Principal Freud called our attention back to him as we moved to depart. "Nice hair, Jackie."

* * * * * * * *

And then we had lunch.

After lunch, it was time to get back to regular classroom topics. Or so we thought.

"Now that we've all had our fill of practical jokes for one day," the McG said, "and that holiday has been dispensed with for another year, what other holidays fall in the month of April?"

We were puzzled.

"Okay, I'm fairly certain it's not Halloween," Petal said.

"Correct you are," the McG said with a sigh. We couldn't really blame her for sighing. Sometimes, Petal had that effect on people.

"It's not Groundhog Day," Durinda said, "or Valentine's Day."

"It's not St. Patrick's Day," Georgia said.

"Thank God it's not New Year's Eve," Rebecca said with a shudder. We knew what she meant. Once your parents have disappeared, or died, on New Year's Eve, you can never look at streamers, funny hats, and noisemakers the same way again.

"Easter?" Zinnia suggested. "Some chocolate bunnies would be nice around now."

"No," Marcia corrected her. "Don't you remember? We had Easter last month, only we were too busy with St. Patrick's Day and . . . *other things* to notice very much."

"I know!" Annie said.

But before Annie could tell us what she knew, Jackie shouted out, "Passover!"

"Ah, yes," the McG said, "Passover. I keep forgetting you Eights are Jewish now. But no, I'm afraid matzo and no bread weren't what I had in mind. Come to think of it, though, I realize that what I'm thinking of is not what most people would consider a holiday at all."

"It's not?" Jackie wrinkled her nose. "Then what is it? What have you been talking about?"

"Tax Day!" the McG said with a big smile.

"*Tax* Day?" Annie asked. "What's *that?*"

"It's something that I have no doubt all your parents are very concerned about right now." Then the McG looked at us Eights, and suddenly she stopped smiling. "Well, *your* parents probably aren't."

This sounded ominous to us, *ominous* being a vocabulary word we'd recently learned that means "foreboding evil."

But we shrugged it off. If this Tax Day was something that concerned adults, then it didn't concern us. Besides which, at least we hadn't been expelled.

* * * * * * * *

Apparently, despite what the McG had said earlier, the foolish craziness and the crazy foolishness of April Fools' Day wasn't done for the year. Or at least, it wasn't done with us.

Okay, so maybe none of us—except Petal—fell for it when the bus driver on the way home claimed we were being attacked by aliens.

But when we got home?

"This really is the limit!" Rebecca shouted to us from the cat room, where she'd gone to clean out the litter boxes. Annie had us on strict schedules to help out around the house, and it was Rebecca's turn to take care of the cats.

Sometimes Annie's chore schedules had fun outcomes, like the time Petal did our first batch of laundry, put in too many soap crystals, and we'd found her swimming in a sea of tiny bubbles. Other times, not so fun.

We followed Rebecca's voice and found . . .

"Now, how in the world did they ever manage that?" Zinnia asked, true wonder and respect in her voice.

All our cats, from Anthrax through Zither, had somehow gotten their paws on rubber dog masks and were staring at us with canine faces.

We could have sworn we heard Jaguar laughing.

* * * * * * * *

And then things got really nutty.

Robot Betty, our black and gold robot who was supposed to clean our house but never did it right, was making love-eyes at the flying watering can, which caused Carl the talking refrigerator to break into tears. Even after Betty made it clear she'd only been teasing him—you know, April Fools'!—it took an awfully long time for Carl to pull himself together enough to let Durinda make us a proper dinner.

"Serves you right," Rebecca said to Carl as she extracted a can of pink frosting from him when it was time for dessert. "You thought jokes were fine enough when you were pulling them on other people. Well, if you can dish it out, you'd better learn to take it."

"Kettle, pot," Georgia muttered.

"Ex*cuse* me?" Rebecca snapped.

Georgia stood her ground. "I only meant that you're a fine one to talk. You're always being . . . *you,* but if anyone acts like you *toward* you, you get all hot under the collar."

Jackie approached the two Eights, placing one hand on each girl's shoulder. "Kettle, pot; pot, kettle. Discuss amongst yourselves."

"Something is very wrong here," Marcia observed out of the blue.

"You mean something worse," Rebecca said, "than robots who never do their jobs properly anyway and talking refrigerators and everyone in the entire world, including your own cats and your own haircutting sister, all playing tricks on you?"

"Yes," Marcia said. "But it's not a wrong something like you're thinking."

"Great," Georgia said. Standing so close to Rebecca for so long was making her as testy as she used to be. "Now you sound just like the McG: 'It's a holiday,' 'No, on second thought, it isn't'; 'It's wrong and worse,' 'On second thought, it's not.' I do wish people would make up their minds!"

"It's just that there's something off." Marcia tried to explain. "I've felt that way all day long. And now, as I'm talking out loud to you about it, I'm coming to realize what that something is."

"Do you think you could tell the rest of us, then?" Annie said, visibly starting to lose patience.

"It's just this," Marcia said. "What hasn't happened yet today that always happens every April Fools' Day?"

What hasn't happened . . . ?

That's when it hit all of us too. Mommy, who was a great scientist and who had created all the inventions in our home, always reprogrammed at least some of those inventions to do crazy things on April Fools' Day. And this year, there had been nothing.

But before we could think any more about that—

The flying watering can came into the room, stopped right over Rebecca's head, and then drenched her.

"Aargh!" Rebecca screamed at the flying watering can. "What are you doing?"

If a flying watering can could be said to smirk, we would have sworn ours was smirking at Rebecca.

Rebecca shook her head, the excess water flying off her hair.

"If I didn't know any better," she said, "I'd say that was another practical joke."

"I wonder if the house has any more tricks up its sleeve," Zinnia wondered. Her eyes danced. "This is kind of fun."

"Maybe for you," Rebecca said through gritted teeth. "I think I'll go to Summer to dry off."

Summer was one of the four seasonal rooms our mother had invented so that we could always go to whatever season we felt like being in at any given moment.

We followed Rebecca, hoping to calm her down, but when we got to Summer . . .

. . . it was snowing!

"*What* is going on here?" Rebecca shouted. "Next thing you know, the sun will be shining in Winter."

Durinda shrugged. "Perhaps we should check?"

When we got to Winter, the sun wasn't shining but yet, somehow, there were flowers growing everywhere.

"This is amazing," Petal said. "Who has the power to make snow fall in summer and flowers bloom in winter?"

"Mommy," Jackie said simply. "No one in the world has that kind of power except for Mommy."

"Do you think she's . . . ?" Annie started to say, her voice hushed, but then she stopped. It was as though she was scared to believe what she was thinking: somehow, Mommy was there.

"No, I don't," Jackie said. "But you know how Mommy is. Always planning ahead for things. She probably set this all up before she disappeared to wherever she disappeared to so that we wouldn't miss her playing tricks on us."

That was Mommy all over: always thinking of us first.

Suddenly, we missed her so very hard; we missed Daddy too. He also always put us first, even if his strength was more in looking good in clothes than in inventing things.

Annie, fighting back tears, clapped her hands together. "Right, then," she said brightly. "Why don't we get our homework done?"

So that's what we did. What else can you do when your parents are still missing, you have no idea where they are, and there is still work to be done?

So we worked, after which we got ready for bed.

We were exhausted now.

"My, this has been one long day," Jackie said.

"It's taken forever to live through it and so much has happened. But I wonder: Do you think a day will come, I don't know when, where it will be one long adventure from beginning to end, kind of like a whole book taking place in a single day?"

Suddenly we were wondering about that too.

And somehow, we knew Jackie was right. It wouldn't happen in April, and it might not happen in May or June or even July, for that matter, but one day, it would happen.

We were certain of that, if nothing else.

CHAPTER FOUR

April 2 passed uneventfully at school, with no practical jokes played or received, but when we arrived home, the little red light on the answering machine next to the phone was blinking like crazy.

We'd stopped answering the phone and turned off the machine shortly after Mommy and Daddy's disappearance because we didn't like always answering calls from telemarketers, but we'd since turned the machine back on because Annie had said it was irresponsible not to. What if someone had an emergency and suddenly needed the help of eight little girls?

"You'd better do something about that," Rebecca said to Annie. "That little red light looks mad."

We still didn't like to actually answer the phone when it rang because we got tired of all the lies we had to tell people: that Daddy was in the bathroom and that Mommy was in France, or vice versa. So we just let the machine catch everything. It was Annie's job to take down the messages, but she didn't usually like doing that because she said no one we were interested in talking to ever called.

This was true. The people we most wanted to hear from, Mommy and Daddy—well, we didn't really believe that that was how we'd first hear from them again. Although we did like to imagine . . .

Hi, girls! we imagined Mommy's voice saying. *Daddy busted his ankle on the runway in Milan, then we got detained in Venezuela when I tried to help the South Americans develop a better postage stamp, but we'll be home soon. Hope you've been behaving!*

It was a nice dream, but we knew it wasn't reality.

As for the other people in our world, our two classmates never called, because we saw them every day at school, and Pete, well, we always called him rather than the other way around. This meant that Annie was right: no one we wanted to talk to would call on that phone.

Annie tried to ignore the phone, just walked right past it.

"I don't think you should ignore it this time," Rebecca insisted. "Look at that blinking red light—the thing looks like it's about to explode!"

And then the phone started to ring.

"Answer it!" Rebecca commanded. We looked at

Annie, wondering if she'd hit Rebecca. Let's face it, no one ever commanded Annie to do anything.

"No," Annie said simply, but she did turn up the machine's volume so we could all hear whoever was calling and picked up the pencil and pad that were beside the phone so she could take down the message.

"Robert?" a man's voice said, sounding both confident and harried at the same time, sort of like if Principal Freud and the McG were rolled into a single person. "Alan Watts here. You do remember me, don't you? Your CPA?"

"What's a CPA?" Petal asked, but Annie shushed her.

"At any rate," this Alan Watts person continued, talking to our father, who wasn't there, "surely you've received the many e-mails I've sent you. Unless they've all disappeared into the ether, as e-mails sometimes do? Although I can't believe that happened to every single one. Still, I've given up on that, which is why I've been trying to reach you by phone all day. You do realize it's Tax Day in just thirteen days, right?"

There were those words again!

Tax Day!

We all mouthed the words. *Tax Day.* What could it be? We'd never heard of it before. Perhaps the McG had been on to something important after all, we thought.

"You haven't hired a new CPA, have you?" Alan Watts said, sounding less sure of himself. "No, of course you haven't," he insisted. "At any rate"—we were beginning to realize that Alan Watts said *at any rate* an awful lot and that it was annoying coming from him— "give me a ring as soon as you get this message." He said his number, and Annie wrote it down. "We'll set up an appointment for you to come into the city. I hope you have all your papers in order. You and Lucy make so much money, and if you don't file your taxes on time—heh, heh, heh—you'll lose it all in late fees. So, at any rate—"

But Annie turned down the volume then so that we wouldn't have to listen to Alan Watts natter on anymore.

"I don't want any part of this . . . *Tax Day!*" Annie cried, throwing down the pencil like it had burned her.

"But I don't think we should ignore it," Zinnia said.

"No," Petal said, her lip starting to quiver. "That man said we could lose all our money. Then not only will we be orphans, we'll be really poor orphans!"

"I think we should call Pete," Jackie said decisively, and she headed off toward Mommy's private study.

"Pete?" Marcia asked. "But why? I mean, he is very nice to us all the time, but I don't think we should be hitting him up for a loan."

"He's our friend," Jackie said, "and he's an adult. He should be able to explain all this stuff about taxes to us."

She picked up the phone and hit the speakerphone button so we could all hear whatever got said.

"What's the number for Pete's Repairs and Auto Wrecking?" Jackie asked Annie.

"Do you really think it's that easy," Annie said with an almost sneer, "to call Pete?"

"Yes, I do," Jackie said. Then she added in a commanding voice, "Number?"

"Jackie has gotten . . . *forceful,*" Zinnia whispered with real admiration.

"I think it must be the hair," Georgia whispered back.

"The number's programmed into speed-dial," Annie said grudgingly. "To call Pete, you just press one."

So that's what Jackie did.

The phone rang two times, then we heard the familiar voice say, "Pete's Repairs and Auto Wrecking."

"Mr. Pete?" Jackie said. "This is Jackie Huit speaking."

"Well, this is a first," Pete said, his voice brightening. "Usually, it's Annie calling. By the way, did I tell you how nice your hair looks?"

"Yes. Yes, you did," Jackie said. "But that's not what I'm calling about. I was wondering, could you tell me, please: what are taxes?"

"Taxis?" Pete sounded surprised, then continued before Jackie could correct him. "Why, taxis are vehicles that people sometimes pay to take them places."

Rebecca rolled her eyes. Truthfully, we all did. It was so rare for Pete to let us down.

"No," Jackie corrected, "not *taxis*. I said *taxes*, as in, um, *Tax Day*. Do you know what taxes and Tax Day are?"

"Oh!" Pete said with a loud groan. We swear, we could almost hear him hitting himself in the head over his own previous stupidity. "Taxes and Tax Day! Now I get it!" He paused. "Except that I don't, not really. Although some people say taxes are one big practical joke played on adults. So, what do you want to know about taxes and Tax Day?"

"Well, it's like this," Jackie said. "What if a person, or *persons,* doesn't or don't pay her or their taxes by, um, Tax Day? Is that a very bad thing?"

"Huh," Pete said. For once, he sounded stumped.

"Well, I don't know. You see, I've always paid all my taxes on time, so it's very hard for me to say."

"*Try,*" Jackie said, using her new forceful tone.

"Well," Pete said, "I suppose I have read about tax cheats. But those are usually wealthy people."

Eight girls gulped in fear. Our parents were wealthy people!

"And what happens to those wealthy tax cheats?" Jackie asked.

"From what I can tell," Pete said, "they have to pay a lot of extra money in fines, or someone comes and takes away some of their stuff as payment, or, sometimes, they even wind up in jail."

"Jail?" Petal shrieked. "But I can't wind up there! I don't want to be a poor orphan in—"

Rebecca would have clapped her hand over Petal's mouth, but Georgia beat her to it.

"Who's that shouting?" Pete asked.

"Shouting?" Jackie asked with a nervous laugh. "Oh, it's just the TV set. Durinda's watching some cooking show and the, um, *French chef* is very loud."

"I see," Pete said, starting to sound suspicious. It was probably because of the word *French.* One day, we were really going to have to come up with something other than France or the French to get us out of tight places. "But what I don't see," he went on, "is why you're suddenly interested in—"

"What are taxes for, Mr. Pete?" Jackie cut him off. "And why do people have to pay them?"

"Why, taxes are used for all sorts of things people need. They're used to keep all the roads paved so that there aren't big holes that could hurt people if their cars hit them."

"Safety," Zinnia said, and Petal nodded. "Safety is important."

"And bridges too," Pete said. "No one wants a bridge to be weak."

"Is that it?" Jackie asked.

"Oh no," Pete said. "There's lots of other things as well. Why, the police, the fire departments—all depend on taxes."

"Those are important things too," Durinda said. "If you have a kitchen fire, you want someone to call who will come and help you."

"And government," Pete said.

"I'm not sure we care about that," Jackie said. "Anything else?"

"Schools," Pete said.

"But that's *insane!*" Marcia, who was rarely outraged by anything, was outraged. "We already pay a huge price to go to the Whistle Stop! We shouldn't have to pay for other schools too!"

"I'll bet it's that usury thing I once told you about," Annie said knowingly, "all over again."

"Hullo?" Pete said. "How many of you am I talking to now?"

"All eight," Jackie admitted with a sigh. "The French cooking show ended, and we're all here now."

"Good," Pete said, "because now maybe you lot can tell me something."

"Yes?" Jackie said.

"Why, Jackie? Why do you all want to know about taxes and Tax Day?"

Instead of answering, Jackie asked, "What's a CPA?"

"It stands for certified public accountant," Pete said immediately, restoring our faith in his brain. "A CPA is a special kind of accountant, and accountants handle filing people's taxes for them. Why do you ask?"

Jackie took a deep breath, big enough for all of us. "Because Daddy's accountant was e-mailing him and we didn't know it and now he's left a million messages on our machine and it's all about the same thing. He says Daddy must bring him his files and, I don't know, whatever else he needs, and then Daddy needs to pay his taxes on time . . . or else."

"Oh dear," Pete said, and then he let out a low whistle. "This can't be good."

CHAPTER FIVE

"This is really bad then, isn't it?" Jackie asked.

"Well, yes," Pete said. "I don't think there's a person in the world who wants the Tax Man after him or her."

The Tax Man. That sounded even more ominous to us than the Wicket, or even the Monster with a Thousand Heads, which was usually Petal's biggest nightmare.

"So what do we do?" Jackie asked.

"We all need to remain calm," Pete said.

Easy for him to say. He wasn't the one who needed to keep Petal from spinning herself off into outer space. At that moment, that was a job for Annie, Durinda, Georgia, Marcia, Rebecca, and Zinnia. Really, right then it was taking all six of them.

"First," Pete said, "you need to locate your parents' tax info, and then you need to make an appointment to see this CPA person and take it all to him."

"That sounds rather involved," Jackie said. "You know, we are all just still seven years old."

"When has that ever stopped you lot from doing anything?" Pete said with a laugh.

That laugh did a lot to lift our spirits. So long as someone could still make jokes, we could tell ourselves that the world wasn't really as scary a place as it seemed.

"Now then," Pete said, his voice turning all businesslike. "I know your dad pretty well. You know, I am the man who works on his cars. And I can tell you this: Robert Huit is a very organized man."

Huh. And here we always thought that the most organized person in our house was Mommy. She was the scientist, after all.

"I'll bet anything," Pete said, "that your dad's just like me."

"But Daddy would never be caught dead wearing a navy blue T-shirt," Zinnia said, but she said it softly so Pete wouldn't hear. Zinnia never liked to offend anybody, except maybe Rebecca. And Georgia.

"And if Daddy did wear a navy blue T-shirt," Georgia said, not bothering to keep her voice low, "he'd find a way to make it look stylish."

Thankfully, if Pete had heard what some of us were saying, he either didn't care or was ignoring it.

"What I mean," Pete said, "is that your dad no doubt has a nice, neat file somewhere, probably marked

Taxes with maybe even the year on it—in this case, you'd be looking for last year's file, 2007—in which he stores all his information."

"And where do you think I'd find such a file?" Jackie asked.

"Two places come to mind," Pete said. "Either in a regular file cabinet or in a file stored in a computer."

We didn't like going near the computer. One, Mommy didn't particularly like them, which we now thought for the first time was kind of odd, given her profession; and two, technology tended to scare us—there was just so much that could go wrong with it!

"I think we'll start with the regular files first," Jackie said.

"Good choice. Okay then," Pete said. "You've got your assignment. Ring me back as soon as you find what you're looking for, and we'll take it from there."

"But don't you have work you have to do?" Jackie asked. "You know, cars to fix?"

"Course I do," Pete said then added, "but nothing's more important than you lot."

Pete may have been a man in a navy blue T-shirt, but he was the best man in a navy blue T-shirt in the entire world.

* * * * * * * *

"Sometimes," Annie said, "I wonder if we rely on Pete too much. I think maybe we shouldn't."

"Why's that?" Marcia asked.

"You don't think Pete's *evil*, do you?" Petal said with a gulp.

"Of course he's not," Durinda said sharply, in a tone she almost never used with Petal. "He's a mechanic and he's our friend."

"I just mean," Annie said, "that I don't think it's good for us to rely on any one person too much. We need to learn to stand on our own two feet."

"Sixteen feet, you mean," Marcia corrected. Good math was very important to Marcia.

"Annie may be right," Jackie said, "and one day we'll have to stand on our own. But that day isn't this day, and now we'd better hunt for the file."

So that's what we did.

The only problem was, the file we were looking for was nowhere to be found. We looked in every file cabinet in the house, we looked in those kitchen cabinets we hardly ever used, we even asked robot Betty if she knew where the tax file might be hiding itself. But if Betty knew anything, she wasn't talking.

By the time we finished tossing the place, our home was a shambles.

"Great," Durinda said. "We're no better off than we were before. In fact, we're worse off, since someone will now have to clean this place and I have an awful feeling about who that someone will be."

"There's only one thing for it," Jackie said decisively. "We'll need to get in that computer."

So we all proceeded with dragging feet to the computer in Mommy's private study. Even though Pete had suspected Daddy was organized, Mommy was the only one who had a computer in the house.

We stared at that technology beast, unwilling to draw close to it.

"Well, Annie," Rebecca said, "aren't you going to take charge? You usually like doing that."

"Oh no," Annie said. "Not this time. Why, Jackie's done so well with taking control of this whole tax problem, I think she should be the one."

Without even taking the deep breath that any of us would have taken before starting, Jackie strode to Mommy's desk and sat in Mommy's chair.

Then she hit the power button on the computer, and the dark screen turned a brilliant shade of red.

That made us jump. The computers at school glowed an eerie blue when they were turned on. Leave it to Mommy to march to her own drummer.

"Okay," Jackie said. "It looks like we need to know the password to get in to see the files. What would such a password be?"

"Usually," Marcia said, "people select words that are important to them."

"Right," Annie said. "It's easier to remember that way. But you don't want it to be *too* easy, because then others will be able to guess it."

"How about Daddy's name?" Durinda suggested. "He's important to Mommy."

Jackie tried typing in *Robert,* but it didn't work.

One strange thing we noticed as Jackie typed: her fingers flew over the keys in a blur. This was odd, because whenever we had to type on the computers at school, we'd all been hunt-and-peck kinds of typists.

"What about trying our names?" Georgia suggested. "I should think we're as important to Mommy as Daddy is."

That didn't work either. Not when Jackie tried the names individually, not when she strung them all together in one long word.

"What about *avocado*?" Petal suggested.

We ignored her.

"What about *Huit*?" Rebecca suggested.

No luck.

"These are all too easy and obvious," Annie said.

"Except for *avocado*," Marcia pointed out.

"Which is exactly why it could very well be—" Petal started to say, but she got cut off.

"I know!" Zinnia's eyes were lit up with excitement. "*Eights!* I'll bet anything the password is *Eights*!"

Only it wasn't.

We were all puzzled, not to mention out of ideas.

But then Jackie's eyes lit up even brighter than Zinnia's, and she pressed one single key rapidly several times.

"What are you *doing?*" Annie asked.

She didn't have to wait for an answer, however, because—*poof!*—we were suddenly in.

"What password did you use?" Marcia asked, always curious. In truth, we were all curious.

"I simply hit the number eight eight times," Jackie said with a smile. "That's us numerically: we're eight Eights."

Once we were in, it was no problem finding the right file. There it was: Taxes 2007.

"Open it up," Annie said.

"Print it all out," Marcia said.

So that's what Jackie did.

"Okay, now close the computer down quick," Petal said, "before something tragic happens to us."

"Not so fast," Jackie said. "I've been thinking lately. Ever since New Year's Eve, we've mostly discovered things—powers, gifts, who's evil and who's not—by events happening to us. Don't you think it's time we took a more active role in finding out what's going on?"

"How do you propose we do *that?*" Rebecca demanded.

"By looking around in Mommy's computer," Jackie said with a twinkle in her eye.

"Oh no!" Petal cried. "That will bring disaster down upon our heads!"

"I say you go for it," Annie directed Jackie, ignoring Petal's cries.

Jackie looked down the list of files. There were so many of them! A lot of them looked like they might be interesting, like the one marked Inventions, but we were still in something of a hurry to get the Tax Man squared away, so we figured we'd save that one for another day.

Then Jackie came across a file marked Persons of Interest.

"Open that one," Georgia said. "We could use some interesting people around here."

When Jackie did, the file contained pictures of three people: a short woman who looked like a toadstool; a pretty, dark-haired woman with an insane look in her eyes; and a man with an egghead.

We knew those three people.

"That's the Wicket!" Durinda said.

"That's Crazy Serena!" Zinnia said.

"What's Principal Freud doing with the two of them?" Marcia wondered.

"He's not with them," Annie said. "Those are three separate pictures. Still, it is odd."

"My, those *are* interesting people." Rebecca's eyes glittered.

"I don't think we have time right now to figure out all the answers to all the questions in the universe," Jackie said. "So let's put this one aside for a while and look at one more file before we get back to those taxes."

Jackie closed that file and returned to the list of other files: Holiday Shopping; Mysteries of Egypt; Things to Do . . .

Zinnia desperately wanted Jackie to open the one called Holiday Shopping. "At least then," she said, "I'll finally know what I would have gotten for a present this year if we'd ever gotten our presents."

"Jackie's not going to do that," Rebecca said, "not if we're only going to look at one more file today."

"But why not?" Zinnia asked.

"Because we won't let her," Annie said firmly.

"Hey," Jackie said, "how about I open this one marked Family?"

"That could be good," Zinnia said, starting to cheer up already. "It'll probably be all about us."

Only it wasn't about us at all. In the folder marked Family, there was a picture of three women: Crazy Serena, Mommy, and another woman who looked almost exactly like Mommy.

CHAPTER SIX

"What does it all *mean?*" Zinnia asked.

"I haven't a clue," Jackie said. "But I'll tell you one thing."

"What's that?" Durinda asked.

"We don't have time for this right now," Jackie said, shutting off the computer. "We have to call Pete back and figure out what to do next about the Tax Man."

"Are you *crazy?*" Georgia asked.

"Excuse me?" Jackie said mildly.

"How can you just turn off the computer at a time like this?" Georgia said, looking like she wanted to punch something. Or some*one*.

"By pressing that little button," Jackie said, indicating the power switch.

"That's not what I meant!" Georgia shouted. "We just saw a picture of Mommy with a woman who looks almost exactly like her and Crazy Serena. We saw a file containing a picture of Principal Freud along with pictures of the Wicket and Crazy Serena. Don't you think it's more important that we focus on *that* rather than *calling Pete about the Tax Man?*"

"No, I don't," said Jackie simply.

"Please explain," Georgia said, tapping her foot, "before I hit something. Or some*one.*"

See? We knew Georgia wanted to do that.

"It's like this," Jackie said. "At the end of *your* adventure month, we started to finally see the pattern of things. We saw that we were getting our powers and gifts in order of our birth, from Annie through Zinnia, with each girl getting her power and gift during the course of a single month. We remembered the original note we found behind the loose stone in the drawing room telling us that we all needed to find our powers and gifts before we could discover what happened to our parents. So we did the math and it finally sank in: we realized we wouldn't really know the whole truth until August, Zinnia's month."

"We did?" Georgia asked.

"Actually," Jackie said, "*you* did. *You* were the one who put it all together."

"I . . ." Georgia looked puzzled, but then a light dawned in her eyes. "Why, yes, that *was* me!"

"You were very smart in that moment," Durinda said

to Georgia kindly. "Really, except for rejecting your gift at the very beginning of the month, you were smart nearly the whole time."

"I really was," Georgia said, looking pleased with herself.

"What's more," Annie said, "we have to keep in mind at all times that we always have *two* problems."

"And those are?" Rebecca asked.

"Discovering what happened to Mommy and Daddy," Annie said, "*and* keeping the rest of the world from discovering that eight little girls are living home alone."

"Because if the world discovers *that,*" Petal said with a shudder, "they will surely split us up and then we will be eight little orphans living in eight separate houses."

"Exactly," Annie said. "And somehow, I don't think we'll ever learn what's really happened to Mommy and Daddy if we get split up."

"So you see," Marcia said, "discovering what happened to Mommy and Daddy is what you would call a long-range problem. But if Mommy and Daddy's taxes aren't paid on time like normal, people will begin to suspect that something is not right here, and then the jig will be up. So dealing with the Tax Man is a more immediate problem."

"Okay, I can see all that now," Georgia said, "and it is nice being reminded of how smart I was last month. But now that we've seen those . . . *pictures* on Mommy's computer, shouldn't we be doing something more *active* to learn what's going on? I mean, even if we know that we won't really know everything until Zinnia gets her power and her gift in August—"

"But Jackie did do something more active," Zinnia pointed out. "It was Jackie who thought to look around more in the files of Mommy's computer in the first place."

"And I'm sure we'll *all* become more active in the search for the truth when we have the time to be," Jackie said, "but right now we have a more immediate problem to deal with, which is exactly what I'm going to do."

Then Jackie picked up the phone again and speed-dialed our man in navy blue.

"Mr. Pete," she said when he answered, "we found the file and printed everything out."

"Excellent!"

"What do we do next?"

"Why, next you call back that CPA person and make an appointment as soon as possible. Then call me and tell me when the appointment is."

So that's what we did.

"Here you go," Annie said to Jackie, holding out the slip of paper with Alan Watts's phone number.

"I must say," Marcia said, "that I'm finding this all rather odd."

"How so?" Annie asked.

"It's just that you never let anyone else take charge of anything," Marcia said, "and now you're letting Jackie take charge of everything. It makes me wonder if, someday, another one of us might not wrest some power from you."

Marcia was the one who was most concerned about power; she had been ever since Annie changed which bedroom she slept in. Marcia was now the youngest in the bedroom with Annie, Georgia, and Jackie, and Annie had put Durinda in with Petal, Rebecca, and Zinnia. Before that, Marcia had been the oldest of the youngest; now she was the youngest of the oldest. We knew she didn't like that.

Marcia's words had a strong effect on Annie, who could also be a little power crazy. Just as Jackie was about to take the slip of paper with the phone number, Annie snatched it back.

"On second thought," Annie said, "I'll call him myself. I only thought to let Jackie do it because it is her month. But really, I should be the one."

Jackie just shrugged. Funny, Jackie didn't seem interested in power at all, in who had it and who didn't, so long as the job got done.

Annie punched in the number and told Alan Watts's secretary that Annie Huit was calling. We supposed she figured that since we were going to have to meet him in person, there was little point in impersonating Daddy now.

"Alan Watts here," a deep voice said.

"And Annie Huit here," Annie said with authority, "Robert and Lucy's daughter."

"Well," Alan Watts said, "it's good to finally be hearing from *someone* in your family at any rate, although I must say, I was hoping it would be your father."

"About that," Annie said. "We've received your messages, but I'm afraid both Mommy and Daddy are, um, out of the country right now and may be for some time, so they won't be able to bring you that information you wanted."

"But that's dreadful news! If I don't file their taxes for them by the fifteenth—" CPA or not, this Alan Watts was working himself up into a Petal frenzy, so it was a good thing Annie cut him off, saying: "But I have the information right here, and I and my sisters will be happy to bring it to you."

"Eight little girls are going to deliver the tax information?" Alan Watts sounded stunned.

"I'm trying very hard not to get offended by your tone," Annie said with dignity. "When shall we bring this to you?"

"How about tomorrow?"

"On a Thursday?" Annie said. "But we can't do that. That's a school day. Same holds true for Friday."

"Fine. Then I'll cancel my golf game on Saturday and you can come in and see me that morning."

"Can you tell me where you're located?" Annie said, pulling out her trusty pencil.

Alan Watts gave her the address.

"At any rate, I'll see you Saturday morning at ten sharp," he said, then hung up.

We all looked at the address in the city.

"How will we get there?" Zinnia asked. "It sounds like a long way away."

"Annie will drive us, of course," Durinda said.

"Oh no, Annie will not," Annie said with a vehement shake of the head.

"But why not?" Marcia asked.

"Because we live in the small city and that's the Big City," Annie said. "I'd need to drive on the highway. I'd need to drive really fast on the highway to get us there." Annie shuddered. "To be honest, I don't think I'm ready for highway driving yet."

"Are you scared?" Rebecca sneered.

"Yes," Annie said simply. "Only a seven-year-old idiot wouldn't be scared of driving a Hummer on the highway."

"Then how will we get there?" Georgia asked.

"The train!" Jackie burst out suddenly. "We could take the train!"

"Oh, that *would* be exciting!" Zinnia said. "It would

be like a real adventure: taking the train into the Big City!"

"But don't trains go really fast?" Petal wanted to know. "I'm not sure I'd like that. Plus, I really don't like the sound of this Big City . . ."

Durinda placed an arm around Petal's shoulders. "We'll all be together," she said, trying to soothe her. "It will be all right."

But when Jackie called Pete to inform him of our plans, it turned out Pete had plans of his own.

"I've decided to take Saturday off," he said. "I'm going with you."

"But why?" Jackie asked. "We already have the file for the CPA."

"Because I want to make sure no one takes advantage of you," Pete said. "Besides, it'll give me another chance to wear my Armani jacket. We can tell Mr. CPA the same thing we tell everyone else, that I'm your uncle.

But as we talked about our plans further, it turned out that we were still in disagreement on how to get there.

"I'll pick you lot up in the flatbed at eight fifteen," Pete said. "Or, since this is a formal business occasion, would you prefer I bring the limo?"

The flatbed? The limo? But we—at least, seven of us—had been looking forward to the train!

"Neither," Jackie said. "Or anyway, not all the way into the city. You can pick us up in the vehicle of your choice, and then you can drive us to the railroad station. You see, we've decided to take the train in, and Petal has her heart set on it, and we'd so hate to disappoint her."

Petal started to protest, rather loudly, but it was too late.

Jackie had already hung up.

* * * * * * * *

It's amazing how quickly Thursday and Friday fly by when you know you are going to see your CPA on Saturday.

Saturday dawned the warmest day yet all year. It was T-shirt weather, and not just for Pete. Except . . .

"We're going into the Big City to meet with our CPA," Annie said. "So take off those T-shirts and put on some more formal clothes."

If Marcia hadn't commented that Annie seemed less concerned with power and control, would Annie be acting less bossy now? we wondered.

Still, we obeyed, exchanging our T-shirts and jeans for dresses and shoes. And we supposed we did fit better with Pete when he arrived, given that he was wearing, as promised, his Armani tuxedo jacket over his navy T-shirt and jeans. He also had on the wide and wild tie we'd seen once before.

The limo to the railroad station was a fun and zippy good ride, but when we arrived at the station, we must say, it was all so confusing.

So many people! Everybody rushing! People here! People there!

"I'll get the tickets," Pete said, and we waited as he went off to buy nine of them.

"Do you think the Big Bad Wolf lives in the Big Bad City?" Petal asked.

"If you promise not to say any more stupid things," Rebecca said to Petal, "we'll let you have the window seat."

"But that might make me feel sick to my stomach and then I might throw up," Petal said. "All the world rushing by my window. *Whoosh! WHOOSH!* It will be so awful—"

"Oh, bother," Georgia said.

"Here we are, then," Pete said in his jolly way, waving the tickets in the air. "Nine tickets."

This *was* exciting! It was exciting because it was a beautiful spring day and we looked pretty in our dresses and we were going into the Big City and each of us was holding her own ticket. Pete was the sort of adult who understood that that was what we would like to do, and so he didn't hold on to them himself as though he thought we might do something foolish, like lose them.

We were feeling so excited and so wanted to be good and behave ourselves properly for Pete that we stood on the platform and waited for the train patiently. Then, when the train arrived, we let the passengers that were on it debark before boarding ourselves in an orderly fashion.

When we walked anywhere, we usually walked in order of age and height, Annie through Zinnia. But on that day, Jackie lagged behind because she was busy pulling up her blue socks. Of all the Eights, Jackie was the one who always had the most trouble with her socks, although we all admit that socks *can* be a tricky thing.

And so it was that Jackie was the last in line to get on, and Jackie was still outside on the platform when a lady came up to her and asked her a question. We couldn't hear what was asked or answered, but of course we saw Jackie's mouth moving and we knew that she was answering, which of course she would, because that is the polite thing to do when someone asks you a question.

But all we could hear was the sound of our own voices shouting out the windows we'd forced open: "Jackie! Please! Hurry up! You'll miss the—"

She couldn't hear us and we couldn't hear her because just then the sliding doors closed, the whistle blew, and the train rolled down the tracks, leaving the station . . .

And Jackie wasn't with us.

CHAPTER SEVEN

We stood at the windows of the train, watching as Jackie in her blue dress grew smaller and smaller behind us. The conductor gently asked us to sit down.

"I don't see you telling the adults to hurry up and sit down," Rebecca objected.

"Yes," the conductor said kindly, "but I just don't want to see you kids get hurt."

"Yeah, right," Rebecca muttered as the conductor moved off to take someone else's ticket. "You're probably just worried about lawsuits."

"Do we even have a lawyer?" Zinnia wondered. "I think it would be nice to have a lawyer."

"We must have one," Annie said. "We have a CPA."

Then, as the train picked up more and more speed, a blue dot zipped by the windows.

"Did you see that?" Marcia asked.

"I've never seen anything like it," Pete said.

"Could it have been a shooting star?" Zinnia asked. "I've always wanted to see one of those."

"I don't think shooting stars fall in the daytime," Georgia said.

"And I'm fairly certain that whenever they do fall," Rebecca said, "they don't shoot sideways like that."

"Could whatever that was be dangerous?" Petal asked. "Do you think we're under attack? You know, our bus driver did say something the other day about aliens—"

"Now let's have no more of this attack talk," Pete said, getting us all settled down into our seats. "Let's just try to enjoy our nice train ride."

But much as we had looked forward to it, we couldn't relax. We were too worried about Jackie.

"I know you must be worried about Jackie," Pete said, reading our minds. "You Eights—or should I be calling you Sevens right now, since Jackie's not here?—have to relax. Jackie is a smart girl. She'll be fine."

Still, we worried. Yes, Jackie was smart. We knew that. But we also knew that she was back there all alone at the train station. She was miles from 888 Middle Way, with no money. How would she get home? Would she wait for us? It would be hours before we got back. We hoped she knew better than to accept a ride from strangers.

"She'll be fine," Pete said again.

Nonetheless, when we looked at him closely, we could tell that even *he* was a bit worried. He reached into the inside pocket of his Armani and pulled something out.

"Breath mint?" He offered the roll around.

So that's what we did for the next hour, we temporary Sevens: knocked back a few breath mints while the

world whizzed by our windows, and tried not to worry about the CPA ahead of us and the Jackie behind us.

* * * * * * * *

The train pulled into the station at the Big City and we all debarked, only to find . . .

Jackie waiting outside the door, leaning against a post

in her pretty blue dress as she casually studied her fingernails.

"What took you all so long?" she asked with a bored yawn.

"*Jackie?*" Poor Pete. He looked like he was about to have a heart attack. "But what . . . ? How did you . . . ? That is to say . . . "

"I think," Annie said in the calm voice of one who knows about such things, "that Jackie just found her power."

"Yes," Jackie said, looking incredibly pleased with herself. "Apparently, my power is that I'm faster than a speeding train."

"That was *you* that zipped past our windows?" Pete asked.

Jackie nodded.

"I'd never have believed it if I hadn't seen it with my own eyes," Pete said. Then he shook his head. "In truth, I *didn't* see it. All I saw, all any of us saw, was a tiny blue dot whizzing by our windows." He thought some more about this, studied us. "Does it always happen like this, when one of you gets her power? One minute you're normal, and then—*boom! bang! lickety-split!*—there it is?"

Durinda shrugged. "Pretty much."

"It truly is amazing," he said, awed.

Eight heads bowed humbly.

Zinnia was the first to recover from our humble moment. "Oh, Jackie!" she said. "What an awesome power!"

"No one will ever beat you again on Field Day!" Petal said.

"I knew when she cut her hair that things were going to change," Rebecca said.

"Well." Pete clapped his hands. "We're all together again. Shall we go see your CPA now?"

* * * * * * * *

Bright lights! Big City!

We liked to think that the place we lived was pretty special, but it was nothing like this.

Everywhere we looked, there were people walking and taxis speeding. Horns blared, and on every corner there was a little metal hot-dog cart.

"Do you think we have time to go see a musical?" Petal wondered. "I think a musical show might be just what I need to calm my nerves."

"'Fraid not," Annie said, not unkindly.

So instead of seeing dancing girls and listening to show tunes, we made our way to the offices of Alan Watts, CPA.

If his secretary was surprised to see nine of us show up for the appointment, she didn't let on.

Alan Watts, on the other hand, couldn't hide his

surprise at the sight of Pete. He stood up from behind his desk and came over to us.

"And who might you be?" he demanded, as if Pete were some stranger who'd followed us in off the streets.

Alan Watts had a body like one long comma, and he had a horseshoe of black hair around an otherwise bald head. His eyes were big and green, the color of money, and they were behind incredibly thick, dark-rimmed glasses. Although he wore a suit, we will say this about Alan Watts: his suit had nothing on Pete's Armani.

"Pete Huit," Pete said, extending his hand for a shake. "Robert's brother. I didn't like the idea of the girls coming into the Big City on their own, so I decided to come along for the ride."

"I hope you had a nice trip in, at any rate," Alan Watts said.

"Oh yes," Pete said. "Why, when we were on that train, you could say that some pretty astonishing things flew by our window."

"Pete Huit," Alan Watts said. "What an interesting name. Did you ever wonder what your parents were thinking when they gave you that name?"

"I can't honestly say I've ever given it any thought." Pete shrugged.

"Are those real glasses?" Rebecca asked Alan Watts.

"Excuse me?" he asked, his eyes growing even more enormous behind the glasses in question.

"It's just that I've never seen glasses so thick before," Rebecca said. "I wondered if they could possibly be real or if this was some sort of practical joke. You know, like April Fools'. And I hear that you play golf. Are you actually able to keep your eye on the ball with those glasses?"

"Please ignore Rebecca," Annie directed Alan Watts. "She's like this with everybody. We do try to keep her under control. But, well, she *is* Rebecca."

Before Rebecca, or any of us, could say something else insulting to our CPA, Annie pulled out the file we'd brought and handed it over to Alan Watts.

He sat down behind his desk while his secretary hauled in seats for the rest of us, since he had only two other chairs. It occurred to us that the secretary worked awfully hard and we hoped she was well paid for it.

"Well, let's see what the damage is," Alan Watts said with a laugh as he opened the file.

We failed to see the humor because we were fairly certain that *damage* never meant anything good.

"I see here that Robert is still modeling and that Lucy is still with SOLSA," Alan Watts said.

SOLSA?

"What is SOLSA?" Annie asked for all of us as we moved to the edge of our seats.

"You don't even know where your own mother works?"

The CPA didn't wait for an answer. "Why, SOLSA stands for the Secret of Life Scientific Agency."

"Then Mommy really is working on—" Rebecca started to say, but Durinda, in a rare act of violence, kicked her.

"And is that what they really work on at this agency," Annie asked coyly, "the secret of life?"

"Oh, I doubt that very much." Alan Watts laughed. "I've always assumed it was just a cover—you know, a ridiculous-sounding name so no one will ever take it seriously or look too closely into what they're doing over at the Agency."

"And what exactly *are* they doing over at . . . the Agency?" Annie pressed.

"Well, I don't rightly know, do I?" Alan Watts said. "Your mother, Lucy Huit, has always been something of a mystery. Really, I am quite certain that even your father would agree with me on *that*."

"First the pictures on the computer back home," Rebecca mused aloud, "and now this . . . SOLSA thing—does anyone else feel like everything we come across is yet another clue? How are we supposed to ever figure out what really means something and what doesn't?"

Sometimes, you just can't get to Rebecca in time to kick her.

"Did you say something?" Alan Watts asked. Thankfully, he'd already turned his attention back to the tax file.

"I said that I really like those glasses," Rebecca said sweetly.

"My," the CPA said after a few moments, addressing Pete as if he were suddenly the only other person who mattered in the room. Some adults were like that, we knew: always thinking that children were or should be invisible. In our family, the only one who really could be invisible was Georgia. And Greatorex.

"Your brother and his wife did very well for themselves last year," Alan Watts said.

"Please address your comments to the Eights too," Pete directed him. "They are here, in case you haven't noticed."

God, we loved Pete.

"Yes." Alan Watts reddened. "As I was saying, er, *all of you,* Robert and Lucy did very well in 2007. In fact, you could say they're my wealthiest clients."

When we'd put the 2007 taxes information into the folder, we'd briefly looked at the sheets of paper. There were lots of numbers on those sheets, but that's all they'd been to us: lots of numbers. None of it meant anything.

But now what we were hearing *did* mean something. We felt that it must mean that our family was rich, even richer than we'd thought.

Who knew a scientist and a model could do so well?

"I'll just keep this," Alan Watts said, putting the folder to one side. "Then, after you leave, I'll run some numbers, call you up with the amount, and send some forms for you to sign and return with a check." Alan Watts looked at Pete closely. "You are authorized to write checks for your brother, are you not, Mr. Huit?"

Pete looked at us, a question in his eyes. He knew a lot about us, probably more than anyone in the world, but he didn't know how we managed our money.

"Oh yes," said Annie, who wrote all our checks, "the Tax Man will get paid."

"Very good," Alan Watts said. "Oh, but I do wish Robert were here. Usually, by this time of year we've already started planning the taxes for the next year."

"I'm afraid that's impossible right now," Annie said.

"Well, then, do you have any idea how much money your parents have made so far this year? At least if I had a place to start—"

"They haven't made anything," Rebecca blurted out.

Georgia kicked her, but it was too late.

"*Nothing?*" Alan Watts was shocked.

"Don't you think they deserve a break from working?" Durinda said hurriedly.

"They've always worked so hard," Marcia said, "too hard."

"And we are incredibly wealthy," Petal said.

"So don't you suppose they deserve a break from the rat race?" Zinnia said.

"I suppose, I suppose," Alan Watts said.

But we could tell that he really didn't understand why people wouldn't make money every second of the day if they could. Well, look at the man. He'd given up his golf game and had his secretary come in on a Saturday just to meet with us.

"Where are Robert and Lucy, by the way?" Alan Watts asked as we all stood up to take our leave.

"Didn't they tell you?" Pete said. "Why, they're in France."

* * * * * * * *

After stopping at a little metal cart for hot dogs, we got on the train. The train ride home was much less eventful than the train ride out had been. We were no longer worried we'd go to jail for not paying our taxes and we had Jackie back with us.

Jackie did say she thought it would be fun for her to race the train home, but Pete was firm.

"I'm not letting you blur out of my sight again, pet," he said.

It was a lot to handle sometimes, we thought, making our way in an adult world, and we were lucky to have Pete with us.

CHAPTER EIGHT

When we returned home, we invited Pete in for a juice
box. We felt we owed him at least that much. After all,
he'd taken us to the Big City, helped us with our CPA,
bought us our train tickets, and even paid for the hot
dogs.

"We've ridden in automobiles and trains since
Mommy and Daddy disappeared," Zinnia said as Annie
unlocked the door. "Do you think planes will be next?
And if so, do you think we'll need to learn to pilot one
ourselves?"

But we'd barely shoved the straws in our juice boxes,
and none of us had had the chance to take even a sip,
when Zinnia shouted, "Jackie! Go check the stone in the
drawing room!"

There was always a note left behind the stone in the
drawing room whenever parents disappeared, or died,
or when one of us found her power or her gift.

Eight of us got very excited then, and Pete tried his

best to look excited too, even though he couldn't really know what this was all about. For a man with salt-and-pepper hair, Pete could sometimes be very good at acting like he was one of us little girls, and now he trotted faithfully behind us as we went to the drawing room.

Sure enough, the stone was loose. We thought that if our life were a mystery book or a mystery TV show, that loose stone would be an ominous sign. Come to think of it, the pigeons that occasionally visited us would be too.

Jackie pulled the stone all the way out and removed the note we all knew she'd find behind it. We crowded around her, looking over her shoulder as she read:

Dear Jackie,

Well done! I always knew you were the fastest in the bunch! Seven down now, nine to go—almost halfway there. Just discover your gift, and you will be. See you soon.

As always, the note was unsigned.

It occurred to us then that the note was right: we *were* almost halfway to discovering what really happened to Mommy and Daddy. This idea made us feel both excited and scared. On one level, we realized that knowing was supposed to be better than not knowing. But on another, we worried: what if the truth was something really awful? That would be hard.

Thankfully, there was Pete, in all his excitement, to distract us from our fears.

"What a *house!*" he said. "Talking refrigerators, mysterious notes." Then his own expression turned a little sad. "Sometimes I wish that I lived in such a place."

"At least you have Mrs. Pete," Petal said, placing a soothing hand on his arm.

"Maybe you could ask her to leave you secret notes," Georgia suggested.

"I don't think it counts as a secret if you have to actually ask someone to leave one for you." Rebecca sneered.

Pete was such a good man, though, he could never be kept down for long, and he cheered himself up almost immediately.

"Say!" he said, his blue eyes brightening. "Isn't it always the case that when one of you lot gets her power, your cat gets the same power? What's your cat's name again?" He snapped his fingers at Jackie. "Jetta? No, that's not it. Jeep? No, that's not it either. Please don't tell me. I've almost got it." He snapped his fingers again. "*Jaguar!*"

Since we wanted to keep Pete looking so happy, we trooped off to find the cats. Plus, we were curious too.

We found the cats lazing around in Spring, licking their paws and their own bellies. Spring seemed an odd room choice, since it was in fact spring, but then we figured that maybe the cats were just very content to live in that season.

The cats had a favorite toy. It was rather large, stuffed with catnip, and in the shape of a German shepherd.

Jackie picked up Biff, which was the catnip dog's name, and hurled his brown and black body across the length of the room.

Seven cats immediately tore themselves away from their life of leisure—Anthrax, Dandruff, Greatorex, Minx, Precious, Rambunctious, and Zither—to chase after Biff. We also saw a tiny gray and white dot whiz past us. When we heard a crash and saw Jaguar leaning against the far wall, Biff in her mouth, we realized that that gray and white dot had been Jaguar. Poor Jaguar. We could almost see the stars swirling around her head; she was probably dizzy from crashing into that wall. Oh well. At least she'd beat the others.

"So now we know," Jackie said. "Our power doesn't tire Jaguar or me out, but running into objects at high speed will always be a risk for us."

"Wow," Pete said. "I suppose this is a real example of 'Hey, kids, don't try this at home.'"

"Or perhaps you should make that *cats*," Marcia corrected.

"I don't think Jackie will be foolish enough to chance running indoors anymore," Durinda said.

"But what if she does?" Petal worried. "What if she runs indoors and she's running with scissors and she runs into me and—"

"I say we take the cats outside to play." Annie cut Petal off.

Our cats were true indoor cats. They didn't usually like to go outside, probably because we made life inside so comfy for them. But on that day, Jaguar seemed happy for the chance to stretch her four speedy legs.

We stood outside at the end of the driveway, still in our dresses and Armani, as Jaguar exercised her new power. She raced a delivery truck and won. She raced a teenager in a little red sports car who was driving far too fast for our quiet little street and won. She even raced a plane flying overhead, and, we would have said, she won. Then she and Jackie faced off against each other, the twin pair of them turning instantly into a blue dot and a gray and white dot.

"Look at Jackie go!" Durinda cried.

"Except we can't really see her anymore, can we?" Rebecca said sourly.

"Why, I'll bet Jackie's faster than a speeding bullet now!" Zinnia said with a happy sigh.

"Too bad she's not more powerful than a locomotive," Georgia said.

"I wonder if she can leap tall buildings in a single bound?" Marcia wondered.

When they returned to us a few minutes later, Jackie declared that it had been a tie. As for Jaguar, if it *hadn't* been a tie, the cat wasn't saying.

"I always knew," Rebecca said darkly, "when Jackie cut her hair and then her cat's, it would lead to . . . *something.*"

* * * * * * *

Back inside, we *still* didn't get to enjoy our juice boxes.

"Mr. Pete," Jackie said, "I was wondering if you'd be

willing to look at something for us, give us your expert opinion . . ."

Seven of us were shocked when Jackie led Pete to Mommy's private study. After years of keeping away from that room, we still found it hard for any one of us to go in, and we'd never invited an adult, although we'd tricked the Wicket into reading a fake file in there.

We all watched as Jackie, with her new confidence, turned on the computer, typed in the password— *88888888* —and located the file marked Persons of Interest.

And suddenly, there was that odd trio of pictures again: the Wicket, Crazy Serena, and Principal Freud, also known as Frank Freud.

"Okay," Pete said, "now I recognize the one in the middle. That's the one who held you lot hostage back in March, the one I had to run out of town for you."

"Yes, that's Crazy Serena," Annie said.

"We think she might be somehow related to Mommy," Durinda said.

"Even if she might be a relative, we are very scared of her," Petal said.

"I can't say as I blame you," Pete said. "Crazy Serena might look great in a turquoise dress, but that is one scary crazy lady." Pete studied the screen some more. "And I recognize the one with the egg for a head. Er,

I mean, the bald guy. That's your principal, Principal Freud, right?"

Eight heads nodded. Of course, Pete was studying the screen right then, rather than looking at us, so it probably didn't matter what we did with our heads!

"Yes," Zinnia piped up. "He runs the Whistle Stop. We like going to school there and hope we never have to stop."

"Not *ever?*" Georgia said.

"Not even when you're *ninety?*" Rebecca said. "You still want to be wearing yellow plaid *then?*"

It occurred to us that Zinnia was probably the only one of us who liked wearing that wretched uniform.

"Now who's this third person?" Pete said, interrupting our thoughts. "She looks like a toadstool."

Pete had never met the Wicket. Perhaps she took her vehicles somewhere else to be serviced? Oh, that's right: she always took taxis. So we explained all about her being the first evil person we'd encountered and had to deal with after Mommy and Daddy had disappeared.

"Or died," Rebecca added.

It used to scare us whenever Rebecca said that, but now we'd come to find it peculiarly comforting. At least one thing in the world hadn't changed and was still reliable: Rebecca's sourness.

"She really does look like a toadstool in person," Marcia said.

"Oh yes," Petal said fearfully, "a poison toadstool. I suspect that if someone tried to eat her, they would die."

"We don't *eat* other people around here," Annie said, for once disgusted with Petal.

"Maybe if I were really hungry, and there was no other food in the house—" Rebecca started to say, but Jackie cut her off.

"Here's the thing," Jackie said. "No matter how much I think about it, I can't figure out why Mommy would have a picture of Principal Freud in the same file with those other two."

"I can," Marcia said.

All eyes turned toward her.

"I've been giving it a lot of thought," Marcia said, "and the way I figure it, this is just like when they have us do Which Item Is Not Like the Others? at school."

"I'm afraid I don't follow," Pete said. "It's been a long time since I was at school. Could you explain?"

"It's this thing they have us do," Annie said.

"They give us a list of words," Durinda said.

"Or a series of pictures," Georgia said.

"And nearly all of them are the same," Petal said.

"Like all fruits or all nouns," Rebecca said.

"Except for one, which is a vegetable or an adjective," Zinnia said.

"And then they ask," Marcia said, "'Which item is not like the others?'"

"Interesting theory, but no," Pete said, looking more serious than we'd seen him all day. "I don't think it works that way at all. At least not this time."

"How do you mean?" Jackie asked.

"It's like this," Pete said. "If Crazy Serena is evil—and she is, I know, because I saw it with my own eyes—and this Wicket person is evil—and you tell me she is, and I believe you—then if Principal Freud's picture is here with these two . . ."

We knew what Pete was going to say even before he said it, but the words were still a shock to hear:

"Then Principal Freud must be evil too."

CHAPTER NINE

This was new and shocking information: the idea that someone we'd known for years, someone who was the head of our school, could be evil.

"What do we do now?" Jackie asked Pete.

"Well, I would think it would be obvious," Pete replied. "Someone needs to get to the bottom of things, find out what's been going on."

We saw that he was right, of course. But how?

Two questions burned in all our minds:

What did Principal Freud know, and when did he know it?

* * * * * * * *

Sunday passed uneventfully, or at least as uneventfully as a day could pass when the day before you'd visited your CPA and later learned there were even more forces for evil in the world than you'd previously imagined.

One thing kept our minds off some of our other problems: the cats. They were becoming a huge problem themselves, what with all the powers they'd acquired.

"I have been talking to them," Zinnia told us.

"Of course you have, dear," Durinda said. Sometimes we wondered at Durinda's endless capacity for humoring the loony among us.

"Are they really planning a kitty coup now?" Petal asked.

"Oh, brother." Rebecca rolled her eyes.

"What are they saying?" Jackie asked seriously.

"Well," Zinnia said, "it's the four youngest who are most upset: Minx, Precious, Rambunctious, and Zither."

"We do know who the four youngest are," Marcia said. We were reminded yet again that Marcia always had a chip on her shoulder because she felt that being the oldest of the four youngest should give her more power, but it didn't.

"They say," Zinnia said, "that it was bad enough when the first three got their powers: Anthrax bossing everyone around, Dandruff freezing the others where they stood so she could eat all the kibble, Greatorex making herself invisible whenever she felt like it. But now with Jaguar being so fast, they are all deeply depressed. They say there's no point in even bothering to chase after Biff when we throw it, because they will never be able to beat Jaguar to the catnip again." Zinnia paused to take a breath. It had been a long speech for her. "They blame it on Jaguar's haircut and say they never liked that haircut to begin with."

"Huh," Jackie said, looking offended at this insult to the haircut. "Well, I don't think they should blame the hair." We knew Jackie was pleased with her own haircut. And who could blame her? Everyone—Pete, Will, evil Principal Freud—kept telling her how nice it looked. "But could you do me a favor?" Jackie asked Zinnia.

"That all depends," Zinnia said, her eyes narrowing. "You're not going to ask me to give you my gift when I finally get it, are you?" Gifts were so important to Zinnia.

"Nothing like that," Jackie assured her. "Could you please tell Jaguar that I, as her mistress, ask that she let the other cats win every now and then when they chase after things?"

We watched as Zinnia whispered into Jaguar's furry ear.

"I can't believe," Rebecca muttered to Jackie, "that you humor the little loony like this."

"Have you ever wondered what would happen," Annie asked Rebecca, "if it turns out that Zinnia is right and that she *can* talk to the cats? The way you treat her, she might one day order them to eat you in your sleep."

That shut Rebecca up.

"Jaguar says," Zinnia told Jackie, "that she is sorry for causing the other cats to be upset. She says she promises to let the other cats win the catnip chases at least half the time."

"Very good," Jackie said.

"She also says," Zinnia went on, "that you should heed your own advice: you should let the rest of us humans beat you at least half the time."

Jackie didn't look quite as pleased about this, but at last she nodded her head. "Point taken."

"Great," Rebecca said. "So now that another kitty emergency has been averted, what are we going to do about Frank Freud?"

It was funny. We'd started calling our former substitute teacher Crazy Serena, rather than Ms. Harkness, after we'd realized she was evil, and it was tough now for us to talk about Frank Freud using the respectful title of Principal. We didn't like to be rude, and certainly not to adults, but what can we say? Cross us Eights once and you are off our respect list.

"We are going to act as cops," Annie said with authority. "We will make him tell us the truth."

"But how?" Georgia wanted to know. "We don't have any guns here." Then her eyes lit up. "Although we do have that spear from Daddy Sparky . . ." Georgia was obsessed with that spear.

"We're not going to use any kind of weapons," Annie said, "except if you consider our wits weapons."

"And we're going to do it ourselves," Jackie said, "without Pete." She nodded decisively at Annie. "It's time we stood on our own sixteen feet."

* * * * * * * *

Since September, the beginning of the school year, we'd done a lot of things around the McG to which her response could best be described as "You could have knocked her over with a feather." We'd put a toad in her desk (Jackie); become invisible (Georgia); and turned out to have a secret life that no doubt both thrilled and terrified her (all of us). But nothing we'd done in the past prepared her for that Monday when Jackie raised her hand in the middle of math and asked:

"Could we all be excused to go to the principal's office?"

The McG didn't exactly fall over, but she did drop her chalk, and it looked like her bun bobbled a bit.

"What?" she said. "But that makes no sense. Students get *sent* to the principal's office, and most students usually try to avoid that. But no one *ever* *asks*—"

"Well, I'm asking," Jackie said. "May we eight go now, please? We have something to discuss with . . . the man who runs this school."

"Fine." The McG turned her eyes toward the heavens and threw up her hands. "Go."

We went.

* * * * * * *

Eight fists knocked on Frank Freud's door. Later on it would occur to us that it must have sounded very odd to him: eight fists knocking. We felt none of the fear kids are supposed to feel when they are about to talk to a Person of Authority. On the contrary. We were excited. We were finally going to get to the bottom of . . . something.

"Enter!" that familiar voice called out to us.

We didn't have to be asked twice.

"Oh!" he said, his eyebrows shooting all the way up to his absent hairline. "You! All eight of you!"

"Yes," Annie said, closing the door behind us with a satisfying *click*. "All eight of us."

"Well, what are you doing here?" He laughed nervously. "Did Mrs. McGillicuddy send you? Are you in trouble again?"

"We're not," Durinda said.

"But somebody is," Georgia said.

"What did you know, Principal Freud," Jackie asked, "and when did you know it?"

"I—" he started to say, but Marcia cut him off.

"You know the Wicket, don't you?" Marcia accused.

"The who?"

"The Wicket," Petal said.

"Short little woman," Rebecca said. "Looks like a toadstool."

"Helena Wicket," Zinnia explained.

"Well," he said, coloring, "I suppose I may have met her once . . ."

"And Crazy Serena," Annie said.

"Crazy who?"

"Serena Harkness," Durinda said.

"Back in March," Georgia said.

"Our substitute teacher," Marcia said.

"Our *pretend* substitute teacher," Rebecca said, stealing Petal's turn to speak. But for once we didn't mind. Rebecca made a good point. So much in our world was pretend, fake—too much, really.

"Yeah. Her." Petal and Zinnia spoke at the same time.

"You brought her here on purpose, didn't you?" Jackie said. "You must have known she was evil and yet you wanted her here. Perhaps it all has something to do with our mother?" She paused, allowing what she'd said to sink in before continuing. "So what I want to know, what we *all* want to know, is: What did you know, and when did you know it?"

Considering how often we'd surprised other people, and considering all the things that had happened to us, it was rare for someone to do something we found truly shocking. And yet that was exactly what happened.

Frank Freud, perhaps feeling like a trapped animal, rose from his chair, stumbled around it, and backed up to the window behind his desk. Then he wrenched open the window, vaulted over the ledge, rushed across the lawn to the faculty parking lot, ran to his reserved spot, which was marked Principal, got in his car, keyed the ignition, and sped away.

And then Jackie leaped out the window—thank God we were on the ground floor!—and raced after him.

CHAPTER TEN

According to the clock, which we started watching when Jackie left, it had been only a half-hour since she'd disappeared, but those thirty minutes had seemed like an eternity to us. It was the first time one of us had faced off alone against one of the evil adults in our world—with the Wicket and then Crazy Serena, we'd all been there together—and we were very worried for her. If Frank Freud had a gun, would Jackie really prove to be faster than a speeding bullet? We'd sat for a lot of tests during our years of schooling, but that was one test we didn't want to see Jackie take.

But then a yellow dot came whizzing toward the open window— "Jackie's plaid uniform!" Zinnia cried— and there was Jackie, fully in the flesh, looking exactly like herself as she climbed over the window ledge and came back into the room.

"What happened?" seven voices shouted.

"Here, sit," Durinda said, pulling out Frank Freud's

chair and forcing Jackie into it. That was Durinda all over: insisting on mothering one of us even while the rest of us—including herself—were dying for news.

Jackie didn't look winded in the slightest, but we must say, she did look wonderful in Frank Freud's big leather swivel chair. It made us wonder if she might be the head of a school when she grew up. It made us wonder what each of us would do when we grew up.

"What happened?" Rebecca shouted. "I want to know what happened!"

"It was really all very simple," Jackie said. "Frank Freud drove to his house, but when he saw me, er, *pull up* right behind him, he grew very scared. Apparently, the idea of us Eights having special powers is terrifying to him."

As Jackie continued to speak, we felt like we were all right there in front of Frank Freud's house. It was almost as though we could *see* what happened, *smell* the fear in him . . .

"I'll ask you again," Jackie demanded as Frank Freud spun around, a look of horror on his face. "What did you know, and when did you know it?"

Frank Freud raced toward the front door of his house.

"I'll sic Durinda on you," Jackie called after him. "You know, she has special powers too. She can

freeze people where they stand. Why, if I ask her to, you just might remain frozen forever."

That froze Frank Freud in his tracks.

He turned to face Jackie, his shoulders slumping.

"Fine," he said. "I'll tell you what you want to know. I met the woman you refer to as the Wicket once, last December. She came to see me at the Whistle Stop after classes had ended but before I'd left for the day. She said she had some questions about your mother. She kept asking if I knew anything about your mother's work, kept saying something about your mother working to discover the secret of eternal life. Well, of course I assumed she was nuts and sent her away. But then, one day, Serena Harkness showed up—I could see the resemblance between her and your mother at once—and she was saying the same things the Wicket had said about

your mother and her work. Then she told me her
plan, to kidnap Mrs. McGillicuddy and try to get
more information out of you Eights. Well, it did
sound a bit extreme. But then I figured, why not? I
mean, who doesn't want to live forever . . ."

"This is all just so odd," Annie said, interrupting
Jackie's recounting of the events. "If Frank Freud didn't
know about Mommy's secret work until the Wicket told
him and then Crazy Serena confirmed it, then why did
Mommy have a picture of him in the same file in which
she kept pictures of the Wicket and Crazy Serena?"

"Who knows?" Jackie shrugged. "Mommy really is a
mystery. But she's also so smart—you know, all of those
inventions, even if they don't all always work. Maybe
she was just keeping a file on greedy people, people
who if they ever found out what she was working on
would become a threat."

"What are we supposed to do when Frank Freud
returns?" Rebecca asked. "Are we supposed to go back
to calling him Principal and pretend none of this ever
happened? I don't think I could do that."

"Oh no," Jackie said. "I took care of that."

"How do you mean?" Durinda wondered.

"I persuaded Frank Freud to take early retirement,"
Jackie said with a satisfied smile. "I believe he said
something about moving to Australia."

As we say, it was the first time any of us had faced an evil adult alone, and Jackie had triumphed.

We were proud of her.

* * * * * * *

"But . . . but . . . but . . ." Petal butted.

"Yes. Spit it out, Petal," Rebecca directed.

"Who will run the Whistle Stop if Frank Freud is no longer here?" Petal asked.

"She's right," Zinnia said. "It would be odd going to a school without a head."

"First Mommy and Daddy disappeared," Marcia began. She held up a finger in Rebecca's direction and directed, "Don't say it!" before she continued; some days, we didn't want to hear that our parents might be dead. "Then we got rid of the Wicket, then Crazy Serena, and now Frank Freud. At this rate, there won't be any adults left in the world!"

"That's a slight exaggeration," Durinda said.

"We still have the McG and Pete and Mrs. Pete," Jackie said.

Annie's eyes lit up. "Say! That gives me an idea!"

But whatever that idea was, Annie wouldn't say at the moment.

* * * * * * *

When we got home from school, a large gray envelope was waiting in the mailbox. The return address read *Alan Watts, CPA.*

"Oh, good!" Annie said, taking it into Daddy's study and getting out the checkbook. "It'll be good to get the Tax Man off our backs."

We gathered round, watching as she signed Daddy's name to the forms and then on a check.

"It seems like an awful lot of money to me," she said, "just to pay for good roads, police and fire people, and other schools."

And yet she didn't look as though she minded at all. It occurred to us then that in the history of the world, no one had ever had more pleasure in paying his or her taxes than Annie Huit.

As if to emphasize this, Annie licked the envelope and then shouted proudly, "We are now officially taxpayers!"

Then she shooed us all out, claiming she had important business to conduct.

* * * * * * * *

By the next day, word had gotten around that Frank Freud had left the Whistle Stop and wasn't planning on coming back.

Our classmates, our teacher—everyone was quite upset.

"But this is just so odd," Mandy said, "Principal Freud just leaving like that. He always seemed like such a nice man."

Leave it to Mandy Stenko to think that.

"It's true," the McG said. "He was always a calming influence whenever I had problems with . . . *certain students.*"

We knew whom she was talking about.

"But I must say," she added, "lately he just seemed so nervous."

"I wonder who the new head of school will be?" Will wondered.

Most of us were still wondering that—the uncertain future was always a big thing to think about—when there was a knock at the classroom door.

The McG called out, "Enter!" and the man who entered looked like a long pencil with a carrot-colored mop of hair. We recognized that carrot-topped pencil. It was Mr. Paul, head of the Whistle Stop's board of trustees.

"Mrs. McGillicuddy, students," he greeted us.

Then he handed the McG an envelope.

We watched as our teacher opened the envelope and pulled out a sheet of paper; watched the shock register on her face; watched her collapse into her chair, stunned.

"Students," Mr. Paul addressed us, "let me introduce you to your new principal."

We would have congratulated her then, but our new principal had fainted, either from the joy or the horror of it all, it was impossible to tell which.

"But I don't understand! We don't understand!" nine voices shouted. One voice remained suspiciously silent.

After Mr. Paul had gotten the McG a cup of water and the McG had been revived, Mr. Paul asked her, "Would you like to read them this letter, or shall I?"

The McG, still too stunned to speak, waved her hand at him.

Mr. Paul cleared his throat, and then he read out the following:

Dear Mr. Paul and the Board,

It has come to my attention that Frank Freud has resigned as principal of the Whistle Stop. Good riddance! I say. But now you will need a new principal. I can think of no better candidate for the job than Phyllis—also known as Hilly—McGillicuddy. As a matter of fact, if you don't make her principal, active immediately, I shall remove my daughters from your school and you shall never see another cent of my vast fortune.

Unlike the notes we found behind the loose stone in our drawing room, this note was signed. And the signature, we saw, as Mr. Paul passed the letter around the room, was *Robert Huit.*

"As you can see," Mr. Paul said, "we really had no choice in the matter. Why, without the Huit money—"

"And without the Eights," Will continued, "the Whistle Stop would be nothing."

"But I just don't see how this is possible," the McG said, looking at us. "Isn't your father in France?"

"He came back briefly before having to leave again," Annie said. Then she flashed a huge grin.

* * * * * * * *

"Well, this is quite a turn of events," Mandy said once we were at recess, the McG safely on the sidelines watching us.

Mr. Paul had explained that even though the McG's appointment as principal was effective immediately, she would go on being our teacher until a proper replacement could be hired.

"I wonder who the new teacher will be?" Marcia wondered.

"I hope she'll be nice," Petal said.

"And pretty," Zinnia added.

"I just hope she's not nuts," Rebecca said with a scowl.

"I wonder what it'll be like to have the McG for a principal?" Durinda wondered.

"Well, she is annoying and only sort of evil," Georgia said, "so it'll probably be okay."

"Sort of anything we can handle," Jackie said.

"True," Rebecca said, "it's only the purely evil that present a problem."

She should know, we thought.

All the time we were debating what the new teacher would be like and what the old teacher would be like as the new principal, Will was practically hopping from foot to foot with excitement. And, like a bag of popcorn in the microwave, he finally reached his limit.

"I can't *believe* you!" he at last burst out.

"What?" Annie asked innocently.

"*You,*" Will said. "*You* are responsible for writing that letter to Mr. Paul and the board, aren't you?"

Annie didn't say anything. None of us did.

"I can't *believe* this!" Will said. "You're all just amazing! You've changed the whole face of this school! You've selected the next principal! Why, you Eights aren't like ordinary humans anymore—*you're kingmakers!*"

Mandy was looking at Will as though he'd gone loony on us. "What is he talking about?" she demanded.

We looked at her, debated, and then saw the time had come.

"Mandy," we said, "we have something to tell you."

CHAPTER ELEVEN

After we'd told Mandy about our parents' disappearance, the fact that we were eight little girls living home alone, and the discovery of some of our powers and gifts, it was her turn to shout "I don't *believe* you!" Only when she shouted it, she didn't mean it in a happily nice way like Will had. It was clear that Mandy Stenko thought we were nuts.

"If you've really got all these special powers," Mandy said, crossing her arms over her chest, "prove it."

"I can file taxes," Annie said.

"Pfft." Mandy tossed her head. "My dad can do that."

"Right. And he's an adult," Georgia said.

"So there," Rebecca added for good measure.

"Maybe you actually need to come over and watch Annie sign checks sometime," Zinnia suggested. "She's awfully good at it."

"*And,*" Petal added, "*she* can drive a car."

Mandy's eyes widened, then narrowed again. "A toy car?"

"No," Annie said simply, "the purple Hummer."

"We put dictionaries on the seat for her to sit on," Marcia said.

"And she wears a Daddy disguise," Jackie added.

"You're next, Durinda," Annie prompted when it became obvious Mandy still didn't believe us about the car; we knew it wouldn't do for Annie to steal one from the parking lot then and there just to show her.

"Who should I freeze?" Durinda asked.

"Do me!" we all shouted, except for Zinnia, who of course couldn't be frozen.

"Oh, please do me!" Will said. "I've never been frozen before!"

We all liked to keep Will happy, so we weren't surprised when Durinda tapped her leg rapidly three times and then sharp-pointed at Will, who froze where he stood.

"Oh," Mandy said, "he's just pretending to be frozen. He always backs you all up in anything you do."

"Try to make him move then," Durinda said with a shrug.

So Mandy tried to move Will's arm, but it wouldn't budge. Then she jumped up and down in front of him like a little maniac, but Will didn't blink. Finally, she pinched him, hard.

Still nothing.

"Huh," she said. "He's even better than those palace guards my family saw when we visited the queen's house in London."

Leave it to Mandy: no matter what the conversation was about, she found a way to turn the topic to all her exotic travels.

After a few minutes, Will came unfrozen, but we could tell Mandy didn't believe he'd ever been frozen at all.

So then, right before Mandy's disbelieving eyes, Georgia twitched her nose twice and made herself invisible.

And for good measure, Jackie turned herself into a yellow dot streaking all around the playground.

When Georgia made herself visible again and Jackie returned to us in full form, Mandy rubbed her eyes. It looked as though her red hair was standing on end.

"I wouldn't have believed it if I hadn't seen it," Mandy said.

"This is our world," Jackie said, "and welcome to it."

"It's *amazing!*" Mandy said. "I've gone to school with you for years and I had no idea. *You're* amazing!"

"Oh," Jackie said with a smile, "you should see what our *cats* can do."

* * * * * * * *

When we got home from school, those very cats greeted us at the door and began circling around Jackie. Jaguar drew close and nudged at her ankles.

"Have my socks fallen down again?" Jackie asked.

"No," Zinnia said. "I think they have something they want to show you."

Seven of us followed behind Jackie as eight cats led her to the drawing room.

And there, draped across the back of a sofa, was a large piece of brilliant red cloth.

Well, we hadn't put it there.

"Your gift!" Zinnia cried. "This must be your gift!"

"I wonder what it is," Marcia said.

"It just looks like a piece of red cloth," Annie said.

"But I suppose it could be a dress," Durinda said.

"Or maybe a really long skirt," Petal said.

"Perhaps it's curtains?" Georgia suggested.

"Well, one thing we know it's not," Rebecca said.

Fourteen eyes looked at her, a single question in those eyes: what *was* she talking about?

"We know it's not a dog," Rebecca said. Then she added "Woof!" for good measure.

"Pick it up!" Zinnia urged Jackie. "See what it is!"

So Jackie picked it up and held it out for all of us to see.

The large piece of brilliant red cloth was a cape.

Jackie swung it wide, then wrapped it around her shoulders.

"It fits perfectly!" Zinnia cried.

Zinnia was right. The cape came to Jackie's ankles. It was neither too long, which is a bad thing in a cape as it causes a person to trip, nor too short, shortness being best avoided in a cape as it makes a person look like she's wearing a capelet.

"Ohhh!" Zinnia said, awe in her voice. "It's *lovely!*"

"You look like a superhero in that," Annie said, not seeming to mind at all that someone else was center stage.

"You look like Superman," Durinda said.

"Except that you're a girl," Georgia said, "and a lot shorter."

"Is there a *J* on the back?" Petal asked, walking around Jackie to look. "You know, like Superman has that giant *S* on his chest?"

"Don't be daft," Rebecca said. "A giant letter would be tacky. You know Mommy and Daddy never liked anything to have monograms all over it."

At the thought of Mommy and Daddy, we grew sad.

"I'll bet they'd both be proud of you," Annie said to Jackie, "the way you handled Frank Freud."

Jackie's eyes filled with tears. It was tough to tell if

she was very happy or still sad; maybe she was both right then.

"Have you all forgotten something?" Rebecca said. "Doesn't anyone but me know what's going on anymore or what order things are supposed to go in?"

Fourteen eyes stared at her again. What *was* she talking about?

"The *note!*" Rebecca said. "Jackie's supposed to check behind the loose stone next. See? It *is* sticking out again! And then she's supposed to read us the note!"

So that's what Jackie did, not just to satisfy herself, but for all of us. Those notes did scare us. Who was leaving them? And how did that person get in here to do so? But those notes also excited us. With each note, with each item ticked off our powers-and-gifts-to-be-gotten list, we knew we were one step closer to learning the truth.

Dear Jackie,

Eight down, eight to go. You've made it
to the halfway point. And, may I say, I'll
bet that red cape looks spiffy on you.

"I would just love," Rebecca said, "for one of these notes to arrive signed one of these days."

"It would be nice to know who's leaving them," Durinda said.

"Or *what's* leaving them," Georgia said, briefly taking over Rebecca's role as the dark one among us. "Do you ever wonder if it could be a monster?"

"Don't scare Petal," Annie cautioned. "Besides, if there were a monster in the house, I should think we would notice."

"Not if it's a really tiny monster," Marcia pointed out.

"True," Annie said, "but if it was a really tiny monster, then I don't think we need to worry about it, do you?"

"It's the monsters you can't see you have to worry about most," Rebecca said. "That, and things changing."

We didn't want to talk about monsters of any kind anymore, because Petal really was starting to look green around the gills, so we decided to do something else instead.

We called Pete to give him an update on our tax

situation (paid) and the resolution of our latest problem with evil (Frank Freud out, the McG in).

"So Jackie found her power and now she's got her gift?" Pete's voice said through the speakerphone. "Lucky girl."

"I think so," Jackie said.

"Now if I understand the pattern," Pete said, "once one of you lot has discovered both her power and her gift, that's pretty much it for adventure that month. Am I right?"

"Pretty much," Jackie said.

"Fine, then," Pete said. "I suppose you're safe for the time being. See you in May."

He rang off.

Then we had an early dinner.

After that, we all headed outside. Jackie, who'd been wise enough to take off her gift while eating, was once again wearing her cape.

Then seven of us stood at the end of the driveway as twilight arrived, the sky turning to gold and purple before becoming a deep blue, and we watched Jackie: her brilliant red cape flew behind her as she walked, and then the whole of her turned into a red dot as she picked up speed and ran up and down our street.

CHAPTER TWELVE

Tax Day was here at last!

The date was April 15, 2008. It was a Tuesday, our birthday was fewer than four months away, we still had Principal McG as a teacher because no replacement had been found yet, Mandy had spent the day looking at us with new respect in her eyes, and we were happy to be home from school.

Happy, that is, until . . .

"That's true, what Pete said, isn't it?" Petal asked.

"Which thing?" Annie asked.

"Don't you find that whatever Pete says, it's always true?" Jackie said.

"I know I do," Zinnia said.

"I'm hungry," Georgia said.

"Is there any pink frosting in the house?" Rebecca asked Durinda.

"I'm not the talking refrigerator," Durinda said. "Why don't you direct that question to Carl?"

"Which thing Pete said?" Marcia asked, recalling us all to the matter at hand as Rebecca left to consult Carl.

"When he said that once whichever of us whose month it is finds her power and gift," Petal said, "then we're all safe from danger for the rest of the month? That thing he said."

Later, we would wonder if it was Petal's insistence on a safe world that caused disaster to fall upon our heads.

Rebecca returned from the kitchen, can of pink frosting and spoon in hand. Ignoring the rest of us, she crossed to the window near the front door and pushed the curtain aside.

"It's such a nice day out," she said. "I wonder if we should play outside before doing our home—"

Then she cut herself off before any of us could, before completing the second part of *homework*.

"Oh no!" Rebecca shouted. "Come quick! Our worst nightmare has returned!"

"What are you talking about?" Annie demanded.

"April Fools' was two weeks ago today," Durinda said.

"So don't expect us to fall for that old 'Come quick!' routine again," Georgia said.

"But I'm serious!" Rebecca said. "It's the Wicket— she's come back!"

"Now I know she's lying," Jackie said.

"We sent the Wicket on a wild-goose chase to Beijing," Marcia said.

"Yes," Petal said, "but we always knew she'd come back one day, didn't we? And she is our biggest nightmare. Of course, we have a lot of biggest nightmares."

"What do you think?" Zinnia asked the cats calmly. "Is Rebecca lying or telling the truth?"

Eight cats raised their furry kitty shoulders and shrugged.

"Would you stop talking to the cats about me?" Rebecca said. "Please come—this is serious. It's the kind of change I *hate,* a change for the worse!"

We don't know why we listened, because we really were sure Rebecca was lying or else needed glasses, but seven of us went to where she was standing, looked over her shoulder out the window, and saw—

The woman still struggling to get her suitcase out of the taxi parked in front of the house next door was an adult, but short enough to be a child, with coal black eyes, a fright of spiky yellow hair, a very plump body, and short legs that looked like they couldn't run fast but could kick hard. The person looked like a toadstool and had on khaki pants and a red shirt with polka dots—no coat. She never wore one, no matter what the weather, and her suitcase was still tied together with a string that didn't look as though it was doing its job properly.

"Oh no!" eight voices cried.

Our evil neighbor the Wicket had returned.

* * * * * * * *

"I never would have believed it if I hadn't seen it with my own eyes," Annie said.

"Me neither," Durinda said. "I could have sworn it was another practical joke."

"Yes," Jackie said, "like all those foolish jokes we were playing on each other two weeks ago."

"Sometimes foolish things turn out to be true," Rebecca said darkly. "Just because something is foolish, that doesn't mean it's *not* true."

"Oh no!" Petal cried. "Does this mean that next the cats will try to stage a coup and take over the house?"

"Earth to Petal," Georgia said. "Remember, the kitty coup practical joke was one Zinnia and *you* made up?"

"Yes, but what if—" Petal started to say, but she was cut off by the oldest among us.

"We need to remain calm," Annie said, "and try to figure out what this means."

"I hate to sound like Petal," Durinda said, "but what *could* it mean other than disaster?"

"Maybe it just means that the Wicket got bored with Beijing," Georgia suggested.

"Or maybe once she realized Mommy wasn't in

Beijing, she figured it was safe for her to come back," Jackie said.

"How do you mean?" Marcia asked.

"I'm not sure," Jackie said with a shrug.

How could she remain so cool? we wondered. Then we remembered: she could now outrun anyone on the planet. Of course she was cool.

"Maybe," Jackie went on, "she decided we can't really do anything to her. Or maybe she's decided to pursue her evil course of action in spite of us. There's really no way to know until we learn more."

"Which is why we should just do our homework right now," Annie said.

"You are kidding us, aren't you?" Rebecca said. "We can't do homework at a time like this!"

"Of course we can," Annie said. "We have to. Our

lives are so far from normal, we have to hang on to the few normal things we still have left."

So that's what we did, our homework, pretending all the while that it was just any ordinary day in ordinary people's lives.

At one point, Jackie went down to get the mail from the mailbox. Through the door, which she'd left open, we heard voices. We followed those voices, looked out the door, and saw that Jackie had run into the Wicket.

The strong smell of fruitcake wafted up to us, making us feel sick to our stomachs.

"Nice hair . . . *Rebecca*," we heard the Wicket say. That was the Wicket all over: she was always getting our names mixed up, as if it didn't matter to her which one of us was which.

"Welcome home . . . *Serena*," Jackie said sweetly.

"Serena?" The human toadstool was outraged. "Why'd you call me that?"

"Is that what you heard?" Jackie said. "But I said Welcome home . . . *neighbor*."

Then Jackie turned smartly on her heel, leaving the Wicket to stare after her as she walked calmly away.

* * * * * * * *

Homework done, dinner done, there was time for life to throw one more "Come quick!" at us.

"Come quick!" Rebecca called from the drawing room.

"What now?" Seven voices groaned.

"The stone is loose again!" Rebecca shouted, sounding almost hysterical.

"Oh, right," Jackie said. "So I'll go in there and I'll pull out the stone and then Rambunctious will jump out at me again."

"I heard that!" Rebecca said. And now she was practically shrieking: "Please come!"

We went.

"And may I remind you," Rebecca said as we entered the drawing room, "that I wasn't lying about the Wicket before."

This was true.

"But I don't understand," Annie said. "Why are you so upset?"

"Because," Rebecca said, "Jackie already got her power and her gift this month, and yet now the stone is loose again. There must be another note in there! But what could another note in the same month mean? Once the second math note comes—you know, the ones that say 'this many down, this many to go'—we don't get another until the next month."

Poor Rebecca. She was gibbering.

"Maybe she's right," Annie said. Then she turned to Jackie. "You open it. It is still your month, after all."

"There just better not be another cat in there," Jackie said, slowly pulling the stone free.

But there was no cat, and there was a note.

The note, that ominous third note, read:

Beware The Other Eights.

Other Eights?

"*What* other Eights?" Jackie wondered.

But before any of us could wonder anything else— and believe us, we were all wondering—something happened.

We heard a sound. It sounded like the wind howling. This was odd. The weather had been very calm that day, not a leaf blowing in the schoolyard, and yet now it was as though there were an enormous storm brewing.

We looked toward the window, expecting to see the trees moving outside. But what we saw instead was a carrier pigeon strike against the glass. More pigeons followed. Then we heard the same sound coming from all around us: wind, almost like thunder, and then those striking noises.

Sixteen feet raced through the house, sixteen feet that now knew they could stand up well enough on their own. We raced from room to room, looking out the windows, witnessing clouds of pigeons strike against the glass.

And then we were in the front room, and now the incredible sounds were striking against our very front door.

It was Jackie who opened the door, Jackie who let the first pigeon in, Jackie who removed the first tiny scroll from the silver tube attached to that first pigeon's leg.

And then there were more pigeons in the house, flying around, and we were all removing tiny scrolls from silver tubes attached to tiny pigeon legs.

But no matter how many tubes we opened and scrolls we read, we always found the same thing:

Beware The Other Eights.

Jackie looked up at us, stunned. We all were.

"*Other* Eights?" Jackie asked. "What other Eights?"